I0548165

BIDDY

S. Wilbur

This book is a work of fiction. Names, characters, places, and incidents are products of the author's imagination or are used fictitiously and are not to be construed as real. Any resemblance to actual events, locales, organizations, or persons, living or dead, is entirely coincidental.

Biddy Copyright © 2017 by S. Wilbur

Cover photo copyright © 2017 by S. Wilbur

All rights reserved.

No part of this book may be used or reproduced or transmitted in any form or any means, electronic or mechanical, including photocopying, recording, or by any information storage and retrieved system or in any manner whatsoever without written permission of the publisher, except in the case of brief quotations embodied in critical articles and reviews.

ISBN 978-0-9971423-4-1

Published by S&P Enterprises

DEDICATION

To my husband Peter

For sharing decades of hugs, laughter and your razor

I look forward to decades more of doing the same

And to my son Ryan

The day you made your entrance onto my stage

the process of cleaning up my act began

TABLE OF CONTENTS

ACKNOWLEDGMENTS

I wish to acknowledge every weird, wonderful, wacky, crazy, wild and free-spirited thinking individual in my circle of friends and family. You have, throughout the course of my lifetime, driven me close to a lovely state of madness.

Either through your encouragement or discouragement, you *all* have contributed in one way or another to my putting my fingers to the keyboard. To protect the guilty, I have omitted your names.

A particularly special acknowledgment goes to my editor, B. J. Harris. Your thirty years of expertise, your keen eye for detail, along with your patience and kindness, combined with our shared experiences as lifelong friends, have all contributed to making me a better writer. Thank you.

Chapter 1

THE DAILY GRIND

Over the years, my working for the Social Security Administration exposed me to meeting my fair share of interesting characters. It happened one day that I met one such character who would change the course of my life in ways I could never have imagined.

That morning started out like most of them did back then. I needed to get my three kids off to school while rushing to get the last of the wet clothes out of the washer and into the dryer. My hope every morning was to accomplish this as well as to feed the dog and let the cat out, all without mixing any of it up. It is true that cats are not nuts about being wet but even more so, they hate being tossed into the dryer. And who would have thought kids could get so prickly when they found dog kibbles instead of cereal in their bowl?

Once these tasks were completed, the next hurdle was to get out of the house and two blocks away in time to catch the local Number 10 bus. Number 10 would take me to the busy downtown corridor which is where I would get off at the corner of South Main and Haddock Streets just in time to catch another bus — the good and loyal Old 32.

Old 32 was always packed full of people from all walks of life. Some were lucky enough to grab a seat before any number of her drivers would accelerate at whiplash speeds — the kind of speeds that could jostle loose the tightest of grips held by the sturdiest and most experienced riders. Everyone, including those seated, would hang on to anything they could. They would brace themselves, some white knuckled, as Old 32 noisily rumbled, bounced and weaved through the predictable, hectic morning traffic.

The air inside Old 32 hung heavy with the scent of soaps and perfumes of the freshly showered and primped masses heading to work. Some odors were far from pleasant, belonging to those of the non-showered. Then again, there were those people whose clothes were permeated with the sour odor of mildew coupled with the stench of smoke from both legal and illegal sources. Add to that concoction the burning scent of diesel smoke which Old 32 spewed out of her soot-covered exhaust pipe, and I was left with a formidable assault on the olfactory zone of my face. Each morning, the potpourri of these odors reached a pinnacle, where I became just light-headed enough to know my stop was coming up. That is when the driver of Old 32 would open her dirty and sticky doors, making my escape possible.

Inhaling a breath of fresh air as big as my lungs could muster (at the very least, the freshest air that can be found in the morning rush-hour traffic), I would find myself at the front steps of a looming and oppressive looking gray, fifteen-story building. This is where the office of the local Social Security Administration was housed, and it was to be my home for the next eight to ten hours depending on the situation. Here, I would perform my duties as an interviewer while advising a myriad of individuals coming in for sundry reasons varying in complexity and urgency. This job had not been my life's goal. It did, however, afford me the capability to put more than just dog kibbles in my kids' cereal bowls.

There were times, while looking down on the city street below, I witnessed all of the people going from one place to another and would have to remind myself, that I once had dreams. It did not matter to me where all these people were going, I was not going anywhere. I sat in the same chair for forty-plus hours a week doing the same thing to the relentless drone of over-and-over. Only the faces changed. Yes, I reminded myself that I had dreams. I would play that over in my head, sometimes to the threshold of depression, and would wonder what happened to me? How did I end up being a watcher and not a doer? *I had dreams — real dreams, damn it!*

One of those dreams was to write. My problem with that was unmistakable; it would not have required analysis from a shrink. It was not that I lacked ideas of what to write about, I had plenty; so many, in fact, I could not narrow them down to make an honest attempt. Then, in addition, there was the pesky and interminable issue of time. The fact that there never seemed to be enough left over after living my life gnawed at me. Between those two major obstacles, I put writing so far out of my mind that, as the years drifted by, I all but forgot about it.

Then, what started out as nondescript as most all of my days had become, I had just finished an interview with a man whose general attitude towards me was one of obvious disdain. I was ready and eager to call the next number in line — Number 221 to be exact.

While I completed the process of clearing this last interviewee's information off the monitor, I saw the small form of an elderly woman out of the corner of my eye. Briskly, she traversed over outstretched legs, around wheelchairs and between and under the arms of much larger individuals than herself, as she made her way to my desk.

Her age was not unusual. She was at the Social Security Administration office after all. However, the combination of her age and the speed at which she approached my desk certainly caught my attention.

Precariously balanced under her left arm were several file folders; while in her right hand, she carried a large, over-stuffed purse. I would learn later that she never called it a purse. It was always referred to as her "satchel." Her actions indicated that she was accustomed to moving quickly. More than likely, this was her normal speed while in her two-legged mode of transportation — something to marvel at for a woman in her advanced years.

Wrapped around her neck was a wool scarf which matched the dark-green wooly hat unevenly plopped on her head; her wavy white hair poked out between the two. The reading glasses she wore — gold and shiny with rhinestones across the top — sat askew midway down her nose, and when she looked at me over them, she flashed an instant, warm smile.

Without rhyme or reason, I knew this day would prove to be different. This one, Number 221, was going to be fun. And as it happens every now and again in life, I was delightfully *not* disappointed.

Chapter 2

BIDDY

Nearly out of breath, shuffling her files into an orderly fashion on the counter without so much as a glance in my direction, she introduced herself as Mrs. Ernst Biddsworth. She immediately made it clear that she preferred not to have a Miss, Mrs. or, God forbid, a Ms. before her name. She did so to comply only with what she called "archaic" and "misogynistic" social standards in place. "My name," she announced with a tilt of her head and a broad smile:

> Should be any damn name *I choose!* My mother wanted to name me Phyliss after her dead mother. My father agreed on Phil. Once he saw I was never going to be a Phil — I didn't have the right parts you see — they compromised on the name 'Beatrice.' Yes, I know the two names are nothing alike, and there's a story behind that. You see —

Mrs. Biddsworth, still adjusting herself and her files, wiggled her petite frame into place:

> Beatrice was a pet pig my father's sister, Lillian, raised as a child. As he told it, he hated my mother's mother, Phyliss. Never got the chance to know her myself, as she had started pushing up daisies long before I entered the picture. My father said he'd wish she'd started gardening long before she did! He never said that around my mother mind you. He said she was always poking her nose where it didn't belong, not my mother, her mother —

Phyliss — just like General Stiltmeyer used to
do. Anyway, my father hated my mother's
mother enough when she was alive, he sure as
hell didn't want to be reminded of her every
time he looked at me. Guess being reminded
of a dirty pig was a better picture.

She immediately followed this explanation with a raucous chortle.

Although I knew instinctively the possibility was nil; for a quick
moment, I entertained the thought that I may be on camera. I took a
furtive look around the room to see if anyone else was privy to this
display. It was apparent everyone was absorbed in their own worlds,
and this little woman and the whirlwind she brought with her was
just for the two of us.

After observation, some would say Mrs. Biddsworth's behavior was
that of someone prone to being scatter brained. This is something
that, I came to understand, there may be an inkling of truth in;
however, I also learned to let go of the concept that having scattered
thoughts was a "negative." Generally speaking, she was in control of
her thoughts and behavior. She would start one sentence opening
one subject which would segue into another, and each topic carried a
valid weight of its own. I came to understand that this was just her
way of being. This was how she conversed, and all of the subjects
she opened — she completed.

Her brain, no different than most of ours, was constantly going. The
difference in her case was that her mouth could almost keep up. No
matter how far afield she traveled in her conversations, she managed
to tie up the loose ends, seemingly not uneasy about the scattered
way her conversations may have appeared to her listeners. She
described her thoughts quite well, I felt, and neatly completed them
on her own terms, in her own way. During our first meeting and in
that initial brief moment, I wondered if she was even aware of my
presence. My question was answered when she stretched her petite
torso over the desk between us and reached for my hand to shake it.
Once our hands were firmly connected she said, "And you, dear, you
may call me Biddy."

Before I could respond, Biddy blurted out, "And what's your name, may I ask?" Without skipping a beat:

> Oh yes, I may, but are you restricted from
> telling me? Now that's the question. Is it like
> at the IRS? I think they can only give numbers,
> no names. Something 'bout disgruntled
> taxpayers. They might look their reps up later,
> and cause 'em all kinds of grief.

Her boisterous laugh immediately followed.

While I shook Biddy's hand and as she sat down, I know I uttered something, though I cannot remember what it was. What I do remember is she immediately looked up at me with a quizzical expression on her face and asked, "Your name is Oscar? Oh dear, you must be pulling my leg. You are kidding me, aren't you?"

Whatever I said, I know for sure it was not "Oscar," but it must have sounded like it to her. I started to laugh and managed to blurt out, "Oh no, no," before I started to laugh harder. "No, my name is not — " Then again, before I could continue further, she interjected, "How rude of me to assume. I'm really very sorry." She carried on:

> That was so rude of me. What if your name
> really was Oscar? People name their kids all
> kinds of weird names. I was named after a dirty
> pig after all! That would be picking on your
> mother. Although —

Taking a quick breath, Biddy continued:

> It could mean something may have been wrong
> with your mother naming a baby girl 'Oscar!'
> Oh dear, there I go again. I don't know if
> something is, or was, wrong with your mother!
> I will say your having to live with that name all
> your life, now that couldn't have been easy.
> But then, maybe it worked out just right for
> you. I mean, here you are working at the Social
> Security Administration and dealing with a lot
> of nutty folks, I'm sure. Some probably forgot

where their nuts are stored, if you get my drift.
My, my, it sure wouldn't be nice of me to bring
attention to your mother being nutty, too, on
top of that, now would it? Wait, now thinking
about it, maybe 'Oscar' isn't such a bad name
after all. It'd be unique for a girl. And, I bet
you are just that — unique. Hmm, maybe I
spoke too soon. Yes, 'Oscar,' not so bad a
name after all.

I was no longer able to contain my laughter; and while getting back
some semblance of composure, inwardly, I thought, "No, my name is
not Oscar." But, did she ever hit the nail on the head in regards to
my mother's mental stability!

What could have been just another routine interview, in a long line of
interviews, turned out to be one of the most enjoyable encounters I
could remember. We spent our thirty-minute allotted time hastily
getting to know each other. Only ten of those minutes were spent
settling the issue that she had originally come in for. She was that
well organized. We found out more about one another than some
people discover spending an uninterrupted month together.

Every topic was interesting, although one jumped out to me more
than the rest. We both found out that we wanted to write. I was not
sure of what I wanted to write about. Biddy wanted to write a book
containing tidbits of advice she had doled out over many years,
solicited or not. "Who knows," she commented, "There may come a
time or two, I could use some of the advice myself."

And so, between Biddy's quick wit, my fits of laughter and the one-
liners that flowed from her with a breezy ease (a knack for humor I
truly envied), we set up a time to meet the following week at her
place. "Be sure to bring your attitude, aptitude and appetite, and I'll
throw lunch together." She concluded, "What don't stick to the
walls, we'll eat!"

While Biddy was gathering her files to leave, I whispered to her, "I
wrote my real name on a stick-it note and put it in your top file."
Her eyes twinkling, she happily replied, "If that works for you
dear — you must know, though, you'll always be Oscar to me."

*****

During Biddy's first meeting with me, we had established (along with
a plethora of other issues) that her name was Beatrice Biddsworth,
and she was married to her best friend Ernst — Ernst Biddsworth.
What I wanted and needed from her in order to help her write her
book was more information — a lot more. Biddy was more than
ready to oblige me and then some. She didn't need coaxing or
coaching. She was filled with stories. The subject did not matter. I
could say "hat," and she would think of an experience sometime in
her past, and inevitably a story would accompany it.

Sometimes, a tidbit of advice would arise somewhere in the midst of
our conversation. I was entertained quite sufficiently with Biddy's
stories, however, I discovered that her advice did not always go along
with the story; although, that had been an integral part of our original
goal. With advice included, or not, the stories in and of themselves
offered more than enough material for me to write about. Biddy
picked up the conversation wherever it fit her. Case in point:

> No shame in having too much, I say. Like
> fixin' food for folks, it's always best to have too
> much. Lot's better than scrounging up sumpin'
> extra, 'specially if you're talkin' the end-of-the-
> day meal. Folks always seem hungriest for that
> meal, I think. Now, where was I? Oh yeah,
> Ernst and me — Oh, wait a minute. Back to
> no shame in having too much to say. I been
> talkin' full-speed ahead for most of my life.
> Surely, all my time with Ernst — fact is he only
> hears 'bout a third of any of it — I can always
> tell when he's not listenin'. He'll swear he is,
> but I know better. He drifts off most of the
> time, but I know how to bring him back.

I asked, "How do you do that?"

> Oh, that's real simple. I say 'foods ready.' You
> ever seen how a dog's ears perk up when they
> hear the word 'treat'? Well, Ernst's face does
> the same damn thing. Sometimes, just for fun,

when I've not even been talkin', I like to say it
just to see his reaction. I tell ya, Oscar, it's the
damnedest thing. 'Hey Ernst, foods on!' And
just like a dog's ears, I tell ya — perks right up,
he does.

At this recollection, Biddy's eyes sparkled, and her face flushed
slightly with an impish, child-like glee. "Yup, we've been married
forty, no, forty-three, or is it forty-five years?" She scrunched her
face up a little at her own question and then answered it with:

After all the falls we've taken, neither of us can
remember. Don't suppose it much matters in
the whole scheme of things. We're still
together and neither of us is going anywhere in
a hurry or at any other pace, for that matter.

I was sure I heard a muffled chuckle come out of her before she said:

Ernst has lots of names for me, you know,
'terms of endearment.' I do for him too.
Couples like us being together more than half
their lives do. I can even repeat some of 'em.

She smiled:

He hardly ever calls me Beatrice. In fact, there
are times I'll hear him refer to a Beatrice while
talking to other people and I'll insist on
knowing immediately, who the hell this
'Beatrice' person is. Then it dawns on me. HA!
It's me! No, he rarely calls me Beatrice. He
calls me Biddy. Like our last name,
Biddsworth, but Biddy for short. And sure
enough —

She claims, clearly beaming, "There are some others that have
another name for me. It starts with the letter 'B' too." Her smile
broadens as a glint of pride crosses her face, "And, I've earned it!"
Changing gears, she started with, "Ernst and I love the tropics. We
go there yearly to thaw out." The rest of the year they reside on an

island in the Pacific Northwest where she swears, "The colder temperature preserves our meat."

For as long as she can remember depending on the time of day you ask her, friends, family and periodically even strangers have requested her advice. In a calm, matter-of-fact tone, she says, "Mostly now, 'cause I look so old, they think I'm wise too! I'll give it to 'em if I feel like it. I've still got some in here." She tapped her forehead with her index finger:

> Truth is, the advice I have and keep giving is
> drawn from a variety of personalities, all living
> in my head. They all got strong opinions too.
> All of 'em. Some are more agreeable than
> others, and every now and then, we all get
> along.
>
> I've always been a note taker, so it came natural
> when my memory started to slip; can't
> remember when, that I started jotting down
> some of the advice I'd doled out. Somewhere a
> long time ago, I started thinking someday I'd
> put it all in a book. Who knows, maybe I'll sell
> it and make enough to get me and Ernst
> matching scooters! No, I think he'd pick blue.
> I'm kinda leaning towards purple with lots of
> colorful, sparkly glitter mixed in it for me —
> yeah, lots of sparkles.
>
> I must of wrote a whole lot of notes, 'cause
> after a while they started filling up the drawers
> in our house. Then, came a point Ernst says to
> me, 'Hey Biddy, you got to do something with
> all these notes. I can't find anything I'm lookin'
> for anymore!' So I ask him, 'What ya looking
> for?' and he says, 'Been too long, can't
> remember now.'

Biddy shook her head and went on to say that, that wasn't the complete truth: "He'd stopped being able to find what he was looking for a long time before the drawers filled up." It was because of these conversations, growing in frequency and intensity, that she was encouraged to seriously address the consolidation of all her notes that she had saved and compile them into a book.

The problem was, as Biddy put it:

> For all the things I'm involved in, along with
> knowing how to type and trying to remember
> what day it is — it makes for gettin' started too
> big a hurdle.

And, as the saying goes, "as fortune, would have it," this is where I came into the picture.

Chapter 3

THE BIDDSWORTH ABODE

Biddy and Ernst's island home sat at the top of a hill at the end of a short road several miles outside of the city in a well-established, quiet neighborhood. From what I could see, there were no two house designs that looked alike. I liked that. Somehow, it fit my expectation of a place where she would live. From what I had witnessed so far, she stood out as quite the individual, unlike most other people I had met in my lifetime.

As I climbed the stairs to Biddy and Ernst's two-story home, I was sure I had figured out how she stayed in such good shape. The climb upstairs provided me with a physical workout, and as I breathlessly reached for the front door, she swung it open. Just as quickly, she turned and disappeared into the living room.

My eyes, blinded by the bright sunshine outside, took a moment to adjust. Before I could see my surroundings, I managed to make out Biddy's tiny frame heading away from me. She called out over her shoulder:

> Come on in Oscar, set your satchel down. I'm
> just burning lunch. And, close the door behind
> you — don't want the flies gettin' out.

As the room became clearer to view, I was intrigued by the combination of contemporary and eclectic styles that unfolded before me. I wasn't sure what I had expected, if anything. I knew only that, so far, the décor of Biddy's home was much like what she had been to me — a surprise!

Although the living room was immaculately cleaned, it was not cold or sterile. Indeed, it was warm, welcoming, and every item inside was well appointed. Dressing the walls were pictures of nature in one form or another and colorful abstract paintings. The tables and shelves had interesting objects neatly placed on and in them. I was curious about them and would spend a good deal of time that first day asking Biddy what they were and where she had acquired them. My line of questioning came about after she had brought to my attention her noticing the expression of surprise on my face which made her ask, "What were you expecting? Doilies? Hate to disappoint, dear — *NO DOILIES FOR BIDDY* — *not now* — *not EVER!*" She did not have a problem making her points clear; and once she did, she obliged me with one story after another, never seeming to run out of energy.

We spent the better part of that afternoon with my asking her questions and she answering them, more often than not, in her story-telling fashion. I realized that, even though the subject matter may have encompassed an array of topics that were far afield from each other, somehow, every subject had a thread connecting it to the others. That thread turned out to be Biddy herself.

One moment, Biddy would be a woman of her advanced age and then, in a flash, she would take on the persona of a young woman — even a child at times. After she told a few stories, it became clear to me that she had no compunction about becoming the character(s) of a man or a woman, old or young — whatever became necessary to complete the story. I was intrigued with her stories and happily engaged in them. On more than one occasion, I found myself breathless just trying to keep up with her.

At just about the time I needed to wrap up our day and head home, Biddy gave me a sudden glance and asked, "Where's your tape recorder?" My face blushed from embarrassment, and I stammered, "I didn't bring one."

Then pointedly Biddy stated, "You must have a fabulous memory. I used to have a good one." She paused a moment and then said:

> But, the years have taken their toll on that part
> of my thinking apparatus. For me, it comes
> down to this: As long as I can remember, I've
> had short-term memory loss!

Biddy burst out with a hardy guffaw. That infectious laugh, I had learned early on, could warm both the room and my heart.

Evening made a surprisingly early arrival; and as I was leaving, Biddy saw me to the door saying, "Great day, Oscar. Think we ironed out the wrinkles. Maybe, we should work on ironin' 'em off my old butt!" Her first comment was in direct reference to our reaching an agreement relating to the approach we had taken in writing our book. Her last comment was just Biddy being Biddy.

We would use a simple interview style: I would ask a question, and Biddy would answer me — simple enough. She had commented, "Folks make things way too hard — a silly waste of time." Thinking back, I don't remember our interviews being in the order that we had agreed to that day — not that it ever mattered.

A few of the "wrinkles" that we had ironed out were that: I would create the dialogue for the interview along with typing and organizing. Biddy would provide the grit and bones of the book. We would use the notes which she had drawers overflowing with — notes which she had jotted down, fearing that she would not be able to remember all of the advice that she had given over the years. She thought that they would be prompts for a later time, when she decided to write her book — not that she needed a prompt to tell a story! Biddy would have free reign to go whichever direction, as she put it, "The wind spits me."

When that time came to be, the wind spit Biddy far and wide — so much so, at times, I lost the interviewer role completely. This situation did not bother me. I had come to enjoy the show I was witnessing, and I accordingly felt comfortable jumping in whenever I felt it necessary to do so.

We had set aside a few hours each week to meet at her place. There, we would encounter little distraction other than from Ernst, on occasion, whom I had not met yet. He was not home when I came for those first few visits. Biddy assured me he would not be a problem, "As long as," she said with a girlish giggle, "I keep him fed."

I knew by this time not to assume anything when it came to Biddy, nor did I want to assume anything: not what her house would look like; not what she might blurt out; and, surely, not what Ernst would be like. I knew, too, that I was eager to find out what kind of man would have spent more than half his life with this woman or, as I was discovering, all the women that made up her personality.

The tone of voice Biddy used when referring to Ernst caught my interest. I came to the conclusion they shared quite a bit of humor in their relationship. And, from what I had experienced from being with her, humor would, in general, play an enormous part of any relationship she was in.

After leaving that night, I understood what the saying "walking on clouds" meant and felt like. I could not remember when I had been more excited about, or eager to start, something new. Although I had never been there before, I recognized that the threshold I found myself at would be one of the most important junctures in my lifetime, both challenging and joyful.

Once back home, I stepped into the shower and savored the hot water flowing over me. It flowed from the top of my head, down through my hair and around every angle and curve of my body. I felt decades of procrastination, coupled with thousands of hurdles that life's circumstances had put before me, now flowing out of and off of me. I then imagined them all being swallowed up by and forever disappearing down the drain.

One last time, I raised my face to meet the warm spray and laughed out loud. It was then that I heard my own voice softy whisper, "Maybe dreams do come true — just maybe, they do."

Chapter 4

LET THE INTERVIEWS BEGIN

We met at Ernst and Biddy's place again for lunch, just as we had done a week earlier. The three of us shared casual conversation, while each of us had a full plate of a variety of vegetables that were sliced and cooked but still firm. They were mixed in with a scrumptious wine and marinara sauce, and then all were poured over penne pasta. This dish was one of Biddy's specialties. She made it clear, too, that she had not gotten any of it on the walls, and that all of it was on our plates instead.

Ernst proved to be as sweet of a man as I would ever meet. Although somewhat quiet at first, he easily engaged in conversation and had quite the wit about him. Seeing the two of them together was delightful. I could feel the comfortable closeness they shared. The presence of their life-long love was obvious, and it filled the room emanating between the two of them — back and forth — from one to the other.

After lunch, Ernst excused himself as he softly thanked Biddy "for another miraculous meal," adding, "I'll be working on a project downstairs if you need me." Biddy piped in, her voice slightly raised, "Be careful Ernst — don't kill yourself." He bent down and gently kissed her on the forehead. She turned away from him with a smile and continued on, "Save that for me to do." Ernst calmly responded, "Of course dear." She watched him walk down the hall and out of sight, then turned to me, "You know, he's the *most* thoughtful man."

Once all of the cleaned dishes were put away, Biddy led me to a beautiful sun room where an expansive view opened up onto and encompassed several pastures in varying stages of new spring growth — beyond that, the waters of the Puget Sound. This was something I rarely got to see and never from the cement walls that enclosed me for over forty hours a week. I could literally feel the view refresh and rejuvenate all of my senses.

The sun room graced on three sides by large picture windows had reached the perfect temperature of warmth from the sun shining through them. There were a few healthy and mature plants which, were easy to see, clearly loved their home. Biddy told me to make myself comfortable, while she kicked off her shoes and invited me to do the same; I complied without hesitation.

There was a sense of belonging in this beautiful place —the sunlight shining in, the plants and Biddy. I looked down and wiggled my toes freely and shared their happy shadows with the warmth of the floor beneath my feet. After consuming our fulfilling and comforting lunch, this sun room was the perfect place to close my eyes and drift off to sleep.

I had less than a moment to entertain that thought, however, when Biddy suddenly stated, "I see you remembered to bring your tape recorder this time, Oscar." Sitting up, now at attention, I eagerly responded, "Yes ma'am, I sure did." I had already pulled it out of my large satchel and placed it on top of the round glass table, which was next to where I had sat down. I was learning.

Biddy proceeded:

> I'm of the mind, Oscar, we turn it on and just
> talk — no formality. We'll keep doing what we
> have been doing all along, we'll have simple
> conversations.

Still standing, Biddy started tending to a few dusty leaves on a tall Ficus tree in the corner, "If we come up with another idea that we think will work better, we can try that too." She put some of the leaves which had fallen off the Ficus tree into her pocket, joining the now dusty tissue she had used to wipe them with. "To start, though, let's just talk. What do ya think of that, O?" I answered, "Sounds good to me. Umm — O? Is 'O' your new nickname for me?" A somewhat surprised expression crept over Biddy's face, "Hmm — "

Biddy stopped tending to her plants, as if she too had heard the name 'O' referenced for the first time without having thought of it until that exact moment, answering, "Sure, I guess so. That is, if you don't mind?" I replied, "No. I mean, no, I don't mind. It's just fine." I could not help but get a kick out of her.

Here I was — getting a new nickname for a name which was not my name to begin with. What, just a few weeks ago would have seemed quite out of the ordinary was now comfortably my new normal.

No, Biddy was not like most people I had met before. In fact, she was not like *anyone* I had *ever* met. I felt special here. She made it that way. I could not put my finger on what exactly it was or how she did it, I only knew that I felt special when I was with her. In a matter-of-fact tone, I responded:

> Yes, in fact, the more I think about it, the more
> I like it — 'O,' that is. Thanks, Biddy. Are you
> ready to begin today's interview?

Back to tending her plants, Biddy answered, "We have dear. We already have."

I reflected on the hundreds of notes Biddy had jotted down and stored away — the quips of advice about this or that which she offered to me as a regular part of a conversation. In doing so, I began to understand that if I was to become the writer I wanted to be, my observations had to be about the whole picture, not just specifics. Ultimately, to that end, everything was an interview; and through that process, I would discover as much about myself as I was learning about her.

Chapter 5

MEDDLIN' MANIAC

Just when I was ready to query Biddy with my first round of
questions, I never got the chance. On this particular day, Biddy came
into the sun room, sat down and pulled some paper from her pocket.

"Oh yes, I remember this one," Biddy said as she smoothed over
what was clearly a piece of crumpled scratch paper.

> I wrote this one some time ago. Quite the story
> as I recall. If I could read it! My eyes aren't
> what they used to be. Don't get me wrong,
> they're still eyes — not ping pong balls!

Biddy giggled, "They just need assistance from my age-paraphernalia
tool. Now, where are my damn reading glasses?" She fidgeted in her
chair, looking between the arm rest and seat cushions. She leaned
first to the left while lifting her leg and then to the right, only to
discover as she patted the top of her head that, that was where she
had left them. "Blast it all, here they are!"

Eager to know what the note revealed, from my vantage point, I
knew I would have to wait until Biddy told me. With or without
assistance from her age-paraphernalia tool, to my eyes, her
handwriting was a mumble jumble of scribbles. Biddy would have to
decipher the scribbles using her beautiful gold-rimmed, rhinestone-
encrusted reading glasses. On occasion, after she put them on, she
would say, "I be stylin'!" I had to agree.

> There was an interesting neighborhood Ernst
> and I lived in many years ago. We were a lot
> younger then. It was filled with young families,
> everybody raisin' kids. And, there were a lot of

kids. We had twins, a boy and a girl, and a boat
load of animals too. Could have said a butt
load, but I really did feel more like Noah back
then, than crap!

Biddy smiled from ear to ear at her comment before continuing:

We had only the two kids, but our neighbors
sure had a lot of 'em. Most had at least three.
One family had seven! Can you imagine such a
thing? Gives me chills just thinking about it. I
often wondered how long it would take folks
like that to figure out what would make that
happen! Anyway, most of the time, a good
number of the kids ended up at our house. We
had lots of toys and games. And with both a
girl and a boy, our toys covered all bases. To
top it off we, Ernst and me, were, well — fun.

As Biddy turned her face to look out the window, I could see by her
expression she was drifting off to another place and time. I could see
only her profile but clearly, she was smiling. Wherever her mind was
wandering, it was a good place. She turned back to look at me and
then to the note in her hand and declared, "But, 'O,' I digress."

After clearing her throat and taking a sip of the sweet, mellow white
tea Biddy had prepared for the both of us, she began again:

You know, I was told I should write a column,
because I shoot straight when it comes to
giving advice. Been told I'm not so sweet when
it comes to giving that advice too. I don't see a
problem with that. If ya ask for it, I'm gonna
give it to ya.

Now *this* note, from what I can read, refers to a
particular neighbor in that neighborhood I was
tellin' ya 'bout. She was an interesting one, for
sure. She'd go from one house to another
picking up tidbits of information and passing it
on to the next neighbor. There wasn't any
good reason for her to do this. Even so, she

took it upon herself to do it. Benign
occurrences in the lives of everyday people,
once passing through her lips, could become
exaggerated stories with deep and negative
innuendoes. She never hesitated to take
liberties by adding to each tidbit a little creative
twist of her own. Nasty ol' crone as I recall.

There was one morning, the one I wrote this
note for where there was a knocking, no — it
was more of a fist pounding — on my front
window. It was her with her full and fleshy
hand leaving greasy hand prints on my freshly
cleaned windows. She was all rattled and out of
breath. I look out to see her cup her hands
over her eyes against my window to block her
own reflection so she'd be able to see inside.

Let me tell ya, if I could of, I'd found a way to
escape out the back. Ernst and I'd gotten
pretty good at that act early on, but she caught
me standing right in the middle of our living
room. There was no escaping. Like a deer in
the headlights, I was. I motioned for her to let
herself in, only as a formality mind you. She'd
already made it to the door, and I could see the
knob turning.

Listen, you can almost hear the scary music
building to a crescendo as the door knob turns
ever so slowly, and the door creaks open. And,
now she's in the house! Like a B-rated thriller,
it was.

She was a crazed woman, I tell ya. Her words
came gushing out of her mouth leaving me little
space to say anything:

> 'You won't believe what those
> three *bitches* up the street are
> saying about me, Biddy! You'd

think after all I do for everyone
here, they'd be at least a little
grateful. *Bitches.* When I think
of the years I've spent helping
everyone out, including with
their kids. You know how
often I've let these ungrateful
parents know what their little
bastards were up to when they'd
come down to this end of the
street. Ungrateful *BITCHES,
Biddy!*

It was during that first moment, O, when I
thought she was taking a breath, I asked her
what exactly they were saying about her.

I tell you, O, her eyes looked like they would
pop out of her sweaty, red face. Half expected
them to shoot out across the room and go
bouncing all over the floor. Bulging they
were — big bulging, crazy eyes. And her
spittle — I could've handled her eyes exploding
out of their sockets, but her damn spittle had
splattered all over my cheeks!

Biddy's description was vivid enough to turn my stomach. Still, I
managed to ask, "Good God, Biddy, what did you do?" "Well, hell,
seeing the veins in her eyes and thinkin' for sure they were 'bout to
pop out, I jumped out of the way!"

Bending over in her chair laughing for a few seconds, she sat back
up:

I'd never really cared much for that woman, but
I did think she deserved to be heard like
anybody, I suppose, so I told her to go on. She
jumped right back in cursing and spewing her
venom, clearly near hysteria now. What
seemed to get her ire up the most was one of
the three '*bitches*' told her they were sick of her

nosey ways, her intrusion into their daily lives
and the peace and calm that was once their
neighborhood.

They didn't see her contributions as helpful.
Nope, they did not. Thought her using
binoculars to peer into their windows was way,
way over the top too! Imagine that.

Another smile crossed Biddy's face, and again, she tilted her head as
if trying to remember something before taking another sip of her tea:

Now mind you, this woman allowed herself a
sense of importance and believed everyone
'round her should have felt the same way.
What she thought was important to pass along
to others was to those on the receiving end a
nuisance, at the very least. And, that's exactly
what she'd become too — an agitating
nuisance — pain in the ol' butt. I know that's
what she was to me and Ernst most of the
time — me, even more so.

I got caught up and pulled into her unyielding
web to listen to her latest ramblings about this
one or that one, more times than I care to
remember. Of course, at this stage of life, it
may actually be more times than I c*an*
remember.

A quick "*Ha!*" followed. I found that this would probably be an
addition to Biddy's commentaries in the future.

Knowing Ernst would have been in the line of fire with this most
unpleasant of women, I interrupted her as I wanted to know how
many times he had fallen victim to this woman too:

Oh no, no, Ernst's an accomplished escape
artist when it comes to anything he doesn't
want to get involved with, and he's the
consummate magician when it comes to his
disappearing act and avoiding the unpleasant.

When I asked how Ernst accomplished that, she simply said, "He excuses himself saying he has to straighten up his workshop."

Upon hearing Biddy's answer, I had to laugh:

> From the sound of it, he'd have had to have
> excused himself quite a bit while living there.
> He must have had a very neat workshop.

Without flinching, even slightly, Biddy looked straight into my eyes and stated flatly, "You'd sure think so, wouldn't ya — that is, if he'd had one."

Feeling a bit uncomfortable with pursuing the condition of, or even the existence of, Ernst's workshop further, I asked, "What'd she do next?"

> Well, as I said, she was beside herself. She
> continued to spew hateful comments. As she
> put it, the ingrates that touted they didn't need
> her, her big nosey nose or her oversized mouth
> around them anymore, were nothin' more than
> ignorant ingrates; and they'd be sorry for
> closing her out.

"Wow," I exclaimed, "She must have said some pretty bad things to have riled up all those neighbors so much."

> Oh yes, she sure did. It seemed that where she
> crossed the line this time, though, was reporting
> that one of these women changed her clothes in
> broad daylight 'where anyone with any decency'
> could see. Oh, the 'impropriety of it,' she said,
> indicating the woman not only wanted to be
> seen, she wanted to put on a little show for the
> viewers to boot.

"Oh no," I answered, "She didn't report this woman to the police, did she?"

> Good Lord, no! She'd have been in real trouble
> if she had. You see, the only way she'd know
> the other woman was changing her clothes was

if she'd been using her binoculars peering into,
like I said earlier, this woman's windows. No.
She was a real pain in the butt, but she wasn't
completely stupid. Maybe just, a little stupid.
Yeah, I'd have to say a little stupid.

She told half the neighbors what she saw, and,
of course, what she thought of it. Not the
brightest light in the chandelier. At times,
barely a flicker there.

After doing the whole neighborhood loop, the
rumor found its way back to the woman whose
privacy had been breached. With the addition
of some colorful, creative license taken by
everyone involved, it had grown into a pretty
sordid story.

I said clearly, "Oh boy, I bet!" Biddy was on a roll, and whether she
heard me or not — it was not initially apparent. She jumped back in:

As it happened, these three women had reached
their saturation point when they decided to
approach this nosey neighbor. They agreed to
give her a 'combined piece of their furious
minds,' as she told it; and to tell her to, in no
uncertain terms, 'take her meddlin' maniac ass
on the long ride back to hell, where she'd come
from!' Beside herself at this point, she was
practically pleading for my advice, '*Help me
Biddy*! What should I do? I'm so upset that
anyone would talk to me that way!'

Raising my eyebrows, I sat back in my chair and braced for what
Biddy was about to say. Upon seeing my reaction, she was quick to
say, "Oh no, O, it wasn't that bad. I simply said, 'Be sure to fill your
gas tank before you go.'"

I proclaimed, "No! You didn't!" Biddy replied:

Yep, yep, I did. Problem was that right after I
said it, I started to laugh. Wish I hadn't —

started to laugh — that is. If I hadn't she might
have got it. My advice was spot on. As it was,
she thought I was making light of it all which
put me on her side. And, you see, there were
no sides for me. I didn't like a one of 'em. Far
as I was concerned, she could have filled the
gas tanks of all those gals' station wagons and
taken the whole lot of 'em, including all their
noisy, sticky-fingered nose miners, back to hell
with her!

Since my mouth had already dropped open upon hearing this, giving
me the appearance of a human fly-catcher, I turned it to my
advantage and asked, "Did you ever set her straight?" Biddy replied,
"Nah, I didn't have space in my life for such hoopla and nonsense
then. I have even less space for that kind of garbage now."

"Well, Biddy," I replied, "guess you could say you did a good thing by
sparing her feelings." She answered, "I am often reminded of how
things would've been better had I got my point across to her."

I ventured — "reminded, how?" Biddy answered, "Every time I get a
letter, you know," she leaned back in her chair and looked up at the
ceiling — "Ernest and I moved out of that neighborhood over thirty
years ago, and that maniac still writes to me!"

Whether she was receiving letters from this obnoxious woman after
all these years as she said, or if Biddy was just having fun with me;
that detail would remain a mystery. My observation of her led me to
believe, her sense of play did not need acknowledgment.

Some people — most people — need to know their ideas, thoughts
and jokes are noticed by those around them. Many would ask, "What
would be the point if others didn't get it?" With Biddy, that did not
seem to matter. It was too early in our relationship to be sure, but I
strongly suspected she was easily satiated and adequately amused by
her own actions without having to have anyone's approval.

In time, I would come to understand that it did not hold importance
to Biddy if anyone was aware of her humor, or if they *got her*. She
was sufficiently successful at amusing herself. The trajectory she
chose, to maneuver her life through, was not dependent on other

people's opinions of her. She forged her own way; and from what I could ascertain, she admitted most anyone on that ride with her. They were just as welcome to jump off at any time; the ride would simply go on without them.

This behavior of Biddy's was foreign to me; as it was commonplace in my world to wonder, if I could come up to what others expected from me. It became apparent to me, that I had been tripping over my own feet throughout my whole life. Hoping to fit in, I tried to meet what I felt were the requirements of others, and I was always asking the questions: Was I smart enough or good enough? Did I say the right things? Was I liked? All of these questions and doubts shadowed me.

Seeking approval was not a passing fancy in my life — it was my mantra. I had to wonder if I would ever be as comfortable in my own skin, as Biddy appeared to be in her's. I knew then, that was exactly how I wanted to be. I came to believe that if anyone's influence could help me achieve a higher level of self-confidence, it would be Biddy's.

Over the next several months, our once-a-week meetings turned into twice a week. Sometimes, they were three-times-a-week get-togethers. I was spending less time at home during my time off. At one point, Ernst and Biddy invited me to bring my family with me to visit them, if they would like to. The opportunity for them to meet each other was a perfect option for me. I talked about them so much, my family felt like they already knew them. And, as I had believed it would be, meeting them worked out beautifully for everyone.

*****

Ernst lit up when my husband, Mike, and our two sons, Jake and Allen, brought their fishing gear. "Now," as he put it, "I've got someone to show off my favorite fishing spots to." Our youngest and only daughter, Bella, loved to "tag along," as her brothers called it — not so much to fish but to find sea shells and sea glass. However, she did show her brothers up on more than one occasion with the bigger catch of the day. When she chose to stay with us,

Biddy included her in whatever she was doing; or we would let her entertain herself, something of which Bella was amply proficient.

Mike and I reflected on how enjoyable it was to spend time with Ernst and Biddy. Sadly, both of Mike's parents were deceased; and mine, well mine were pretty well burned out from years of drug use. I never knew what to expect from them. On the one hand, I had hoped they would come around to see their grandchildren; on the other, I was glad they chose not to be involved. The last thing I needed was for one of them or the other to teach my kids how to roll a joint. If they were going to learn how to do it, they would have to learn to do so on the street from their friends like any other kid — not from good ol' Grandma and Grandpa.

Biddy and Ernst offered all of us a sense of extended family, and our lives felt more fulfilled in their presence. I wanted to give back to them, and my completing Biddy's book was on the top of the list of priorities for doing that.

As I continued to tape Biddy's and my conversations, I would also play them back and listen to the recordings, I had already taped. Then, I would listen to the new ones and take notes. I would write and rewrite, and then rewrite again.

My commute to work had become a blessing of sorts. Working on the book helped me to take my mind off of what the other passengers were doing and saying. Only once in a while, my concentration would be interrupted, such as the time I heard a little boy ask, "Mommy what's this brown thing?" To which she screeched her reply, "Drop that immediately William, and I mean *NOW!*"

Over time, on my commute to work, I had witnessed the trimming of toe nails, the picking of ears and, for whatever reason, a disproportionate number of people pulling their underwear out of their derrières. This always made me wonder, "Don't people know what size underwear they should wear?" I had seen, heard and smelled more than my fair share of folks performing any number of bodily functions which were just short of a cause for arrest. Many of their actions were disgusting, and most of them were best left unmentioned. After a great deal of observation, I had come to a well-earned opinion: Being engrossed in writing Biddy's book was clearly a better choice than being grossed out.

The drudgery of my commute had all but disappeared. Strangely, I found myself wishing it were longer, so that I could finish just one more sentence before arriving at my stop. There, I would find myself having to shut down the process until my trip back home. On one hand, that was frustrating; on the other, it gave me something to look forward to.

Chapter 6

TO SLEEP OR NOT TO SLEEP

"Oh, O, I'm sorry. I must have fallen asleep for a minute."

Clearly confused, I commented, "But Biddy, your eyes were wide open."

Yep, they were. It's a trick Ernst taught me. He told me, it really helped him back when he worked and had to sit in on long meetings. Sometimes, now, it just happens when I don't mean for it to. Other times, it really comes in handy. I've found it particularly helpful when anyone wants to show me their new baby pictures or, God forbid, their vacation slides.

Ever know anyone, O, that possess the overwhelming compulsion to share the pictures of their summer vacation with you? I've got a piece of advice for you, if you do.

We knew a family that took hurried, family vacations every summer. It was the oddest thing, really. The husband would pack the kids, his wife and the dog into the car and take off. He sped out of his driveway so quickly, you'd a thought they were being hurried into the Witness Protection Program. His wife said he'd drive at speeds only known to meteorites. And, while flying down the road, he'd tell her to take pictures of the sights, as they whizzed by them. Just imagine that. Sounds like so much fun, don't it!

Biddy snickered and stood up long enough to stretch, as if she *had* just awoken from a nap. I was still wondering, "Had she been pulling my leg; or had she, indeed, been asleep with her eyes open, when I came into the room?" I have to admit, it was a little unnerving to observe. Even, still, I doubted if I would ever know for sure. She once told me that she loved leaving people in a state of wonder. She said, "That was when we do our best thinking." If this was true, I must have been in a state of deep thought most of the time since meeting her! She explained:

> I can't tell you how many summers I tried
> avoiding the annual slide show of objects that
> were so blurred, it looked like nothing more
> than drops of watercolors blown across paper.
> Every now and then, I could identify a
> recognizable partial, human forearm bracing
> itself on the car door above the open window.
> But mostly, in the midst of the watercolors, I'd
> see a portion of the side mirror. Not much else
> was discernible. No — wait a minute — there
> were a couple of times, his wife wouldn't roll
> down the window. Yeah, I remember her
> telling me that.
>
> The wife would sometimes keep the window
> rolled up for fear the camera would blow out of
> her hands, and she feared she'd get hit by a bug.
> If she was right about the speeds her husband
> was driving, a bug hitting her would be like
> getting hit by a bullet. In place of lead
> fragments pummeling her, it would be the bug's
> sticky innards splashing with such violent force
> that deciphering the difference between its guts
> and the vulnerable flesh of her face, arm and
> hands would be too difficult to do. In those
> shots, I'd get a glimpse of her reflected,
> contorted face along with a stretched out image
> of her camera — all swirling in a mix with the
> watercolor portrait — that begged the question,
> 'Why in the hell are you doing this?'

For some reason, these folks never minded the paint-blurred photos. They'd all pipe up and say in unison something like, 'Isn't that where Eddie Joe lost his lunch?' And laughter would ensue.

'Yeah, sure is.' Another family member would say, 'Just after Mile Post 24, near the giant ball of twine!' They would go on and on about how great it was to visit the giant ball of twine. Then, one of them would compare it to cousin Jeffrey James' pile of fishing line that he had been building up in his backyard. It was inevitable someone else would seriously suggest that Jeffrey James put up a sign to lure people passing by, to pay a fee to see it. 'He'd probably make a whole pile a money from that pile a fishin' line,' another would interject, and they'd all laugh again.

Then there was the time this family wanted to show me pictures of Jeffrey James' 'pile a sumpin.' It was in the farthest part of his backyard, down by the creek. No one knew what was in the pile — thus the name. Here, I stood my ground and said, I'd seen quite enough pictures, thank you. *My* visiting the pictures of that 'pile a sumpin' would just have to wait for another, unfortunate circumstance I'd find myself in.

Still, Eddie Joe, the youngest of the brood, throwing up all over his sister's dress won out as the more memorable event. They'd all get a good laugh, especially Eddie Joe. His older sister — I think her name was Alice, yes, Alice Mae — well, Alice Mae didn't seem to want to live there anymore; and, I often got the impression she wasn't getting the same pleasure out of the memories that her six brothers and parents seemed to get. She often looked to me

as if she was drifting off to another place —
probably dreaming of being a member of
another family. That would be my best bet. I
know if it was me, that's exactly what I'd be
dreaming.

I'll tell ya, O, after sitting through a hundred or
more slides and listening to that family
reminiscing about stories like that, summer
after summer, I found Ernst's tips on 'how to
sleep with your eyes open,' a true blessing. Oh
yeah, and I also learned how to drink white
lightening without throwing up. Have to say
after a shot or two of that — then, and only
then — did those goofy-ass pictures make any
sense!

I laughed so hard at Biddy's story, my sides hurt, but it was a pain I
could easily adjust to. If for no other reason, it was accompanied
with the best side effects — a high better than drugs could offer and
a come-down of pure joy.

As Biddy put it, she saw that she had three choices: One, take a
motion-sickness pill to endure the event without getting sick; two, get
blasted; or three, fall asleep with her eyes wide open. Her advice for
anyone finding themselves in this same, or similar, unpleasant
situation would be to choose number three — falling asleep. That
was the best choice for the health of one's liver, and the fact that
sleeping with your eyes open is just plain scary looking; it would keep
a good number of people away (which could only add an extra layer
of incentive). She then added with a wink, "Besides, you can get
blasted any ol' time."

Chapter 7

A HOT TOPIC

Ernst quietly came inside from doing yard work hiding his hands behind his back. He approached Biddy, and when he exposed his hands, he was holding two small, beautiful roses. The expression on his face was that of a sweet boy who had just picked for his young love, her favorite flowers. Her face lit up causing his face to beam in return. She thanked him and then stood up taking them from his hand. He bent down as she stood on her tiptoes, and gently their lips touched. I felt a little embarrassed, almost as if I was peeking into a place I shouldn't be looking. It did not matter though, as neither one of them seemed to be aware that I was even on the planet, let alone, in the room with them. I tried to busy myself with the tape recorder just to keep my eyes from looking at them.

I could not help but wonder how Ernst and Biddy could make a kiss look like the most romantic gesture one could display, especially after being together for so many years. I felt envious of their connection with one another. They made love look so easy, just as I had always believed it should be. At one point, Biddy shared with me:

> With all that couples have to do to make a life
> together, sometimes they overlook just why
> they are doing it together to start with. Don't
> forget that, dear, and you'll be fine.

Biddy made loving sound so simple.

By all standards, Mike and I had a good marriage. I knew we loved each other, but we did not quite have the glow that Biddy and Ernst did. How did they still have it after so many years? What could we do to get it back (if we ever even had it), or how could I make it start for Mike and me now?

34

Biddy told me that loving Ernst was nothing she *had* to do, and that it was easy to love him. Making it clear to me in her own way, she said he had not been the first man she had loved; although, he would be the last. "Call it what you want," she told me. "Whatever it is I feel for him, I've never felt for anyone else. I'll be married to this man for as long as I live," Biddy reaffirmed.

To me, Ernst and Biddy's affection for one another always seemed to fall right into place. She let me know there were times, that was not always the case for them. For instance, on those occasions when he would offer to help put the dishes away; she swore he would put them in the wrong place on purpose, just to hear her say, "How the hell long have you lived in this house?" She was sure he did this, so that the next time he offered to help, she would yell, "Don't you dare! I'd like to eat again someday, and I'll never find anything to eat off of if I let you in this kitchen!"

Biddy relayed to me that Ernst would say in a hurt tone, "I was only trying to help." She knew better, proclaiming, "I know passive-aggressive behaviors when I see 'em!" Her voice was raised and unyielding, "No, there were times things didn't always fall into place." But, seeking common ground never ceased to be their goal.

I piped in, "I wish all issues were that simple to solve between couples." She reassured me:

> They could be. Like I said earlier, couples
> make it harder than it ever needs to be by
> losing sight of *why* they are making a life
> together to start with. Maybe the fire's not as
> hot as it once was, I mean, not as often. All the
> embers need is a little stir. That's it. They'll
> ignite all over again. I know that's true with us.

Ernst may have been too tired over the years, on occasion, and Biddy too. But, that was when she would make an extra effort. "There were times that man begged me to wait until the next night," she giggled like a naughty school girl, "But I couldn't. I'd wait until he had a couple hours of sleep and then make my move!"

"Your libido must be more active than mine," my response was blatantly candid and honest. She responded:

> See now, that's just the thing I'm talking about.
> I'd run our schedules over in my head and
> realize it'd been longer than I'd like it to have
> been. For him too, I was sure. If we kept
> letting our busy schedules get in the way, we
> might be able to get in a five- or ten-minute
> rush job, but it could be a long time before we
> felt the radiant heat from those embers, if you
> get my drift.

I got her drift alright. Mike's and my "embers" had been buried under a pile of cold ash lately. It was not something either of us talked about, and it did not seem like anything was going to change in the near future, not in the direction Biddy was referring to. Our schedules were so busy, neither of us had enough energy at the end of the day. A kiss goodnight was about all we could manage, or had managed, for quite some time. And then, when we did find time, it was quick — wonderful, yes, but quick. We needed more time together, more than the five- or ten-minute "rush job" she referred to. Biddy advised:

> It's not all about that, O. Enough of it is, and
> couples should pay attention to it. You won't
> always swing from the chandeliers, but don't
> become so complacent that you overlook the
> staircase to get there!

As far as Biddy and Ernst's relationship goes, as a whole, she said it felt natural to be together and foreign to be apart. Whatever fate that may have befallen them, including actual falls, they assured each other that they would be there with ice for the other one's bumps for as long as they were able.

*****

Biddy sat down in her favorite chair in the sun room, the room that had become my favorite room *anywhere*. This day was especially glorious. It had been raining for what seemed like weeks. That morning, we finally got a break; and the sun's rays were dancing off every object they touched, spreading their glittering prisms of color everywhere. I sat across from Biddy, right at the spot where the sunlight shown through all of the windows at once engulfing both of us in a life-affirming embrace. Relaxing there, I felt I had been away for some time and had finally come back — not just back — I had come home.

Biddy and I sat in silence for a few moments sharing the gift that particular morning was, when she calmly said, "Sex, O, sex." Jolted from my calm, my less-than-intelligent reply was, "Huh?"

Biddy replied, "You've got the boys and little Bella. How do you think you'll tell them about it, sex that is?" It was not her question that caught me off-guard. I found my mouth teetering on words that were still trying to form by a brain that was not yet up to speed. And, it was not that I had any qualms talking about sex, I was okay with that. The truth was, after having been around her for so long, her question surprised me less than how I reacted. Anyone who knew Biddy knew to expect the unexpected. "Silly me," I thought, and then replied, "Honestly, Biddy, I don't know." Calmly, Biddy pushed on:

> I didn't mean to be nosey, O. I just wondered what parents are doing today to introduce their kids to the subject. The subject of sex is everywhere, you know. It's used to sell just about everything from clothes to roofing materials. That's true. Just about everywhere, I think. Here, in our country, it comes with such a mix-mash of messages. And, everybody has their own way of reasoning why their ideas are the right ones.
>
> I think our society has got it all screwed up. Sexual innuendos pop up everywhere. Hell, forget innuendos — that's too subtle. You can't go to a grocery store without seeing half-dressed men and women splashed all over the front pages of magazines with headlines saying things like, 'Joe Blow is sleeping with Mary Whistle while they're both married to some other windbags.' And there's the constant barrage of newer and better ways to do what

we've been doing since the beginning of time.
Boldface headlines glare out at you while you
pull your head of lettuce and bag of tomatoes
out of your cart, 'A hundred new ways to please
your partner in bed.' A hundred, O! My, my,
don't know how they found out what Ernst and
I've been up to all these years!

After this rant, Biddy heartily laughed:

To me, there's a time for everything, and by this
time, all I want to do is pay for my groceries
and go home to make dinner!

Ernst and I have never read a book to figure
out what goes where or in how many angles it
works. The sex sellers go too far if you ask me.
Takin' sumpin' natural with the right partner is
an excellent way to spend a Sunday, thank you
very much, and they've turned it every which
way. Hmm — thinkin' on it — Ernst and I
have been quite the acrobats on occasion.
There are some delightful techniques if you're
flexible enough.

Biddy laughed again, looking in my direction where I sat with the sun
and shock on my face. Was she just messing with me? Again, I
would never know. What I did know was that for the next few
weeks, every time I saw Ernst, I would divert my eyes and feel my
face blush. Totally unaffected by my shocked expression, Biddy
continued:

Yep, we're pretty screwed up when it comes to
sex, as a society that is. We advertise it and *use*
it to advertise. Haven't seen one yet, but
wouldn't be surprised if one day I see a
commercial with some young beauty and her
hunk walking hand in hand on the beach —
their firm backsides swaying seductively. Then,
picture it — as the camera pans down —
there's toilet paper hanging out of the back of

their skimpy swimsuit bottoms. I can hear it now, the narrative would go like this, 'Whatever you do together, keep it clean!' Selling sex and toilet paper together, now there's an idea. All of *this,* while at the same time, there's so much controversy over sex education and birth control. Someone explain that to me! Let's not talk straight out about it. And let's not talk to our kids about that! Hell, we don't need to tell them about sex; they see and hear about it *everywhere, every day!*

*****

Stiffy drug advertising, O. Barely a night goes by when Ernst and me are eating dinner; when there it is, some commercial pushing Stiffy drugs.

My voice came out an octave or two higher than I was familiar with, "*What?*"

You know, for limpy's the opposite of a stiffy. Now and again, that issue may arise for a man. I stand corrected. It's the *not arising* that's the issue! You see commercial after commercial advertising drugs men can take to remedy this. One, in particular, puzzles me.

There's a man and woman in separate bathtubs out in the middle of nowhere. They're holding hands watching the sunset or sunrise, hell, it's one or the other. Again, they're in the middle of nowhere, so I have no point of reference as to east or west. If they're trying to keep rhythm with the theme of the advertisement, it's probably rising. Anyway, the narrator is going on about getting it right or being right for the moment. I may be mixing one commercial up with another — don't matter, they're selling the

same stuff, just a different name — all going
for the same goal.

Mind you, they've just got their point across, in
that their stuff will get the man's stuff stiff for
the occasion. Then, they start in with the
warnings. Poor guy, he finally gets his stiffy,
and then he's warned of all the things that
could go wrong. I mean, here's this poor guy
that finally has what he's been hoping for, and
then he could very well end up in the
emergency room with a stiffy he can't get rid of.

Picture it, O. He's done his business as many
times as he could, and as many times as his
partner would. I can hear it now. 'Come near
me again, and I'll drop ya with my shotgun!' she
shouts. And there he is. A stiffy all at the
ready and nowhere to go — kind of like
General Stiltmeyer used to get. It was
downright embarrassing to my good ol' mother.
She'd say, 'Ben, please do something with the
General. He's got his pink shiny out again and
we've got company coming!'

This time, I had to interrupt. As best as I could recall, this was at the
least her second reference to this "General Stiltmeyer," and I had no
idea who he was.

"Biddy, I apologize, but I have to ask, who is this General Stiltmeyer
you keep referring too?"

Oh, no need to apologize, dear. He was a big
Great Dane we used to have — a wonderful
dog. I thought he was my pony for the longest
time. That's what my dad told me, and hell, I
believed him. Had many wonderful years with
him. And, now that I think of it, my dad too!
He tended to embarrass my mother.

"General Stiltmeyer, or your father?" I queried.

Both, but then a lot of things did — embarrass
her, that is — especially my dad. Anyway,
guess that saying, 'be careful what you wish for'
would ring a little too loud for this guy — the
guy with the limpy who now has a stiffy. The
happy in that message is really short-lived.
Meanwhile, this couple continues to hold hands
while in separate bathtubs for God's sake. It
ticks me off to no end.

Adjusting myself in my chair, I asked, "What part ticks you off the
most? The warnings or the couple in separate tubs?"

All of it, the whole blasted thing. Guess the
worst part is their treating us like we're stupid.
We're talking about gettin' a stiffy for Christ's
sake. Why in hell do they have these folks in
bathtubs out in the middle of nowhere anyway?
And anyone with half a brain knows, if ya have
problems getting a stiffy in the first place, your
best shot at getting one would be to have the
both of ya in the *same damn tub*!

At Biddy's response, I had to laugh. She made a good point, actually
several. We do see sex in advertising every day, so much so, that we
don't even think about it. It has become engrained in our heads as
common place. She took a breath before continuing:

I really get myself in a twist when it comes to
the hypocrisy of it all. At the same time these
commercials are shown on how to get the man
to rise to the occasion, a whole bunch of folks
say 'no' to sex education. Let's do all we can to
entice everyone to be doing the humpity hump,
but don't dare tell them how to do it safely.
Tell me, when was the last time you saw a
commercial about how to get the ol' limpy to
rise to the occasion?

I did not take long to arrive at my answer. "To be honest," I said,
"probably last night."

Yeah, and when, pray tell, was the last time you
saw some commercial advertising
contraceptives or suggesting the use of
condoms to help stop passing disease or
preventing an unwanted pregnancy? Somebody
has got to tell folks. Sometimes, you gotta take
seriously, somethin's being poked in fun! Give
me a break. Gets me riled up, O.

"I can see that, Biddy, and have to agree. It makes little to no sense
the way we tiptoe around the issue of sex," I replied.

Then Biddy said, "And all the while, they use it to sell anything from
cars to toilet cleaners. And everywhere you look, titties."

My voice cracking, I asked, "What?" Biddy answered:

Titties. They're everywhere. Can't miss 'em.
They're in our faces all the time. We're just so
used to seeing 'em we don't think about it
much. Here a titty, there a titty — 'course
they're young ones, not ol' hangers like mine. If
they were like mine, folks would be tripping
over 'em. Yep, trippin' titties. Sounds like the
name of a rock group from the sixties.

At this latest rant, Biddy and I both let out hardy laughs.

You ever notice how you see titties and
women's butts all over the place. Not as often,
you'll see a man's butt and rarely, if ever, his
dangly. Not that I have any desire to see a
man's dangly. If I wanted to see one of those,
I'd have no further to look than my Ernst. He's
pretty much been obliging in that area. Not a
modest bone in his body when it comes to just
us being here. Since he retired, he's gotten to
be even less so, modest that is — not that he
ever was, like I said. Sometimes, I see him
during a time of day he should have his pants
on, and he doesn't. So I ask him, 'Ernst, where
are your pants?' And he says, 'there in the

fridge!' I tell ya, O, he's a real comedian at times. Even so, with all the titties and butts all over magazines, TV, and in the movies; you'd think an open, honest conversation about sex education wouldn't be an issue.

What are folks so afraid of? Do they think there'll be gangs of hormonal youngsters searching the wilderness for empty bathtubs they can get themselves into trouble in?

Scoffing, Biddy carried on:

Of course, if they do like they do in the commercial, they'll be okay cuz they'll be in separate bathtubs! Mind ya, I don't begrudge parents teaching their kids about it as long as that's what they do. It's when they tell their kids some unrealistic stories about how it all works.

If ya ask me, setting *unrealistic* expectations sets everyone up for *real* failure. Preparing kids for the real world and real consequences for their actions is where I'd like to see more emphasis placed.

I tell ya, O, we're a society of split personalities when it comes to sex. Yep, we are. We'll sell it, or use it to sell, all the while pretending not everybody's doing it! Believe me, if they're not doing it yet, they're just about to. And, God forbid, we tell the truth about it.

Biddy's voice was elevated now, and at the tip of its crescendo, she stammered, "Sex, Sex, SEX!!!"

"In a little bit, dear" — we heard Ernst pipe up from the living room. My face heating up once again, I could not help but think my circulatory system was in better shape, since I had started visiting these two. Biddy turned to me and asked, "So, O, how do you think you'll handle it?"

This was not the first time, I had tossed the idea over in my head of discussing the subject of sex with my children. As a parent of young children, it is something I knew Mike and I would eventually be faced with. The initial discomfort of Biddy's bringing it up to me had passed as I spoke:

Well, my hope is to be honest — as honest as I can be. I have to keep in mind their age and give information that they will be able to understand — you know, information that is age appropriate.

I took a deep breath in and calmly let it out. Now, I felt comfortable and assured that my composure had returned. Biddy then asked, "Do you think any of them have seen you and Mike having sex?" So much for composure — I thought my jaw would hit the floor. "Oh God! I don't think so. No, no, I can't even think of such a thing. No, nope — God, I hope not!"

Biddy looked directly at me, unable to contain her laughter:

>It wouldn't be the end of the world, O. I
>walked in on my parents when I was about
>seven, and I managed to make it to this late,
>great stage of life with barely a life-lasting scar
>from it!

Now, Biddy laughed hardily:

>Yep, I was about seven, I think. It was on a
>Saturday morning. I'd been awake for a while.
>My dog had jumped up on the bed which was a
>big 'no no' in my house. It was my parent's
>rule, not mine. I'd sneak him under the covers
>with me every chance I'd get. Mind you, this
>dog wasn't General Stiltmeyer, he'd have
>broken the springs! Anyway, I knew if my
>parents knew I snuck this little dog under the
>covers, I'd get in real trouble. That's why I
>stayed awake and very quiet.
>
>I remember hearing something that didn't
>sound right, and so I listened very carefully. It
>wasn't something I could identify, but to me, it

> sounded so out of place. The sound peaked my
> curiosity. It started getting louder and louder,
> like someone was having a hard time breathing.
> And, it started to scare me.

Biddy's story was a story I was pretty sure I did not want to hear. I
was still dealing with the urge to shake my head as hard as I needed
to get the picture out of my mind's eye of my kids standing at the end
of Mike's and my bed, their big brown eyes agape in shock. By now,
though, I knew Biddy well enough to know that once on a roll, she
would keep going until she was distracted. Even so, she would find
her way back to finish whatever she had started:

> After putting my dog in his bed, I slipped
> quietly out of bed and tiptoed down the hall to
> my parents' room. The closer I got to their
> room, the louder the sound became. Their
> door was ajar just enough for me to peek
> inside. I wasn't sure of what I was seeing. I
> was seven after all. I knew the people I saw
> were my parents, but I'd never seen them in
> this way before.

Biddy noticed the expression on my face and remarked, "I can see
this is upsetting to you, O." I replied:

> Not really. Well, maybe a little, but only
> because I am having a hard time getting the
> picture of my kids' expressions — if they were
> ever to walk in on us — out of my head!

Biddy continued on:

> Yes, O, I can fully understand where you are
> coming from. I think of the decades that have
> passed since that unfortunate Saturday
> morning. That picture is engrained in my head.
> I've forgotten a lot more than some will ever
> know, and yet, that image remains clear in my
> mind.

The sounds I heard that morning drew the
courage out of me to find out what was causing
them. I was afraid, really. Not knowing what
was causing them, I chose to go find out
instead of calling on my parents to do it. I
wonder why it was on that particular day that I
mustered up courage, as I was a pretty timid
child.

Surprised, I queried, "You, Biddy, timid? I have to readjust my
thinking cap again for that one!" She answered:

Don't let this smart-ass mouth of mine or my
bad attitude confuse you. There was a time
when I was as timid as a mouse, scared of most
everything, too. That's why I find it curious,
that I would go looking on my own for the
cause of those sounds on that particular
morning.

When I peeked into their room, I saw
something I'd never seen and heard sounds that
I'd never heard. Somehow, I knew instinctively
I wasn't supposed to be there. I quickly turned
and made my way back to my bed. And,
speaking of mice, at that point, I was quieter
than any one of them could ever be.

It was then, I heard my father say to my
mother, 'I think she saw us. I'm going in there
to see.' My mother said something like, 'Ben
don't. I'm sure she didn't come in here.' I
could hear him open the door to their room
and then he started to stomp down the hall.
Talk about the fear of God!

Back under the blankets, I froze in my bed. My
heart was beating so loud in my ears, I was sure
anyone within hearing distance would hear it
too. I tried holding my breath and tried not to
swallow. My heart pounded harder the closer

his steps came. Just before my head and chest
exploded, my body forced an involuntary intake
breath, and my chest rose and lowered out of
my control. I turned on my side and pulled the
sheets over myself holding my arm just enough
above my torso, so my rising chest wasn't
visible.

Biddy sat back in her chair, looking as if the memory had just made
her blood pressure rise. I know mine had. Taking shorter breaths
now, she said:

My father pushed open my bedroom door and
came directly to the side of my bed, where I
laid as still as death. 'Beatrice! Beatrice!
BEATRICE!' His voice was as stern as I'd ever
heard it, and I was terrified. I knew — again,
due to that instinct thing — I needed to act as
if he'd just woke me up, so I moved slightly and
mumbled, 'Huh?' He sharply asked, 'Were you
in our room?' My acting had to be perfect to
get through this. For a terrified seven-year-old,
I'd have to say I did a pretty good job of pulling
it off. I muttered sleepily, 'Huh? What Daddy?'
I immediately breathed deeply, as if I'd fallen
back to sleep; indicating, I'd never truly
awoken. In reality, my lungs were dying for
nourishment, and the deep breath gave them a
glimmer of hope, that they and I would survive.

It wasn't more than a second or two, I'm sure,
but it felt like fifteen minutes of the purest fear
from hell, before I heard him turn and leave the
room.

I remarked, "Oh Biddy, that must have been awful for you, especially
being such a young child."

Biddy replied, "Well, it wasn't a day at the beach, I can assure you —
toilet paper hanging out of my bottoms or not!" We both burst out
with laughter.

My thinking on this subject was a good place to pull us back to her advice on this delicate matter. I pursued, "So, what would you advise parents to do, to open the doors on the subject of discussing sex with our children?"

The force of Biddy's laughter pushed her back into her chair as she countered, "Don't — Keep 'em closed, and for God's sake, lock 'em too. No kid wants to see that stuff!"

Hmm, it appeared to me, Biddy may have just got me again. It was becoming clearer that, perhaps, I may have been taking this all a bit too seriously.

Chapter 8

POLITICS AND OTHER STRANGE
BEDFELLOWS

In addition to my parents' issues with drug use, my family found it difficult to listen to, or to be open to, the opinions of each other. That, in and of itself, caused a lot of tension and resentment.

The atmosphere in the Biddsworths' home was totally different. I felt like I could say what was on my mind and not be judged. They were a lot like Mike is with me. Even when I knew they were not in total agreement with my idea, they made me feel that — although my idea was different than theirs, it was not only okay, but I was welcomed — no, encouraged — to express it. That took a little getting used to, and it helped me to feel a little more at ease when approaching Biddy on subjects such as her stand on controversial issues like politics and religion. She had already made it clear to me, that she had no compunction when it came to discussing sex.

Our Country's election that year was winding down towards the end of a long bid for the presidency, when I thought it would be interesting to get Biddy's take on the process.

"So Biddy," I asked, "You've seen your fair share of presidential elections in your life, what do you think of this one?"

Biddy's response sounded like "Umph," followed by, "Not so much fair, but a whole hell of lot of 'em, for sure."

I questioned, "Did any compare to the one we're having right now?"

Biddy replied, "There was a time I thought they couldn't get any worse."

Half-jokingly, I quickly interjected, "Do you mean the process itself or the candidates?" "Both!" she snapped. "Don't mean to be so nasty, but the whole mess makes me madder than a wet hen," she snarled.

Biddy was not one to shy away from expressing her point of view, and this political subject clearly had her riled up. Just then, Ernst came into the sun room; and in a tone as gentle as the touch of his hand on her shoulder, he asked, "We're not going to have to stop watching the news again, now are we dear?"

Biddy, almost as gently, removed his hand from her shoulder, as she readjusted her position in her chair replying, "Don't you worry yourself, Ernst; the only thing that might happen is I'll scar poor O beyond repair." "Scar or scare?" he queried. Biddy laughed, "Both!"

At Biddy's response, Ernst patted her on the shoulder and turned to leave the room. It was then that he turned to me, and with a wink, he said, "Buckle up."

*****

I was well into my trip home that night, before I recognized how exhausted I was. All of the time I spent with Biddy consumed my interest. After a full day with her, I left knowing I would sleep well, the way one does after a good day of hard work; although, I never looked at the time we spent together working on the book as real work. This particular day was, by all descriptions, more entertaining than most. As I put the key into the front-door lock, I reflected on one particular comment Biddy had made:

> It's all how you look at it. And man-o'-man, is
> there a hippo-sized pile of ways to look at it!
> When people say 'back to the ol' grind,' some
> think of work — some think of sex — I'm
> thinking, teeth. Maybe, it's just me. And when
> it comes to politics and politicians, I can size
> the whole mess up into one big, stinkin'
> shebang. And, this time around 'taint a tad
> different — no, that's not completely true.
> This time 'round, it's a whole hippo-sized pile
> worse!

I interrupted, "Now Biddy, if you are not going to tell me what you really think, well — " She shot me back a look — not one that I would say reflected the humor in which I had presented the comment. Then, she slightly tilted her head in my direction, and I recognized the tiniest glimmer in her eyes as she remarked, "I'm embarrassed this time around — even more than usual." Biddy's voice had taken on a more serious tone now as she continued, "What kind of a mess we're in for, I don't know yet. But, it's gonna be a mess for sure."

Without pronouncing which side of the political spectrum I leaned, I had to agree with Biddy, that this election had been a particularly contentious race. "It's left us more divided than we were when the campaigning started!" she quipped.

Just then, Biddy's cell phone squealed. This, being the first time I had heard it, I jumped up in my seat which made us both laugh instantaneously. She pulled it from her sweater pocket to see who was calling and made another "umph" sound:

> Now, even these phones get the unsolicited
> callers! Wish I knew how to make a special
> ring-tone, as they call 'em, to let me know when
> it's one of 'em. Nothing would make me
> happier than to just blow a whistle in their
> damn ears!

> Ernst set it so it'd make this sound for me
> when anyone calls. He said it'd be the same
> sound my tires make when I'm pulling into the
> driveway.

Biddy's cell phone ring-tone sounded just like the squealing a car makes while making a very sharp turn at a high speed. Picturing Biddy pulling into their driveway at such a speed, I was convinced, beyond any doubt, that I would be the one driving us if the need should ever arise. It was then Biddy declared:

> All these confounded new gadgets today, I'm at
> a loss how to use 'em. Take this phone — used
> to be, even before me — out in the country
> let's say, there were few enough people; they

only had to use an operator to get to the person
or place, they needed to call. Sometime later, a
thing came along called the 'party line.'

"A what?" I asked. Biddy answered:

> A party line. Don't know exactly how it
> worked — from a technical point, that is. Just
> remember that if you had a party line, you
> shared your phone with other people.

"That's odd," I replied, though somewhat intrigued by the idea. I was
happy it was no longer in practice. Biddy explained:

> Not sure how it all started. I think it was
> supposed to make the use of the phone
> available to more people. Spreading the
> charges over a number of subscribers made it
> that more financially feasible. Makes sense, I
> guess, from that point of view.

Retrieving a cloth from within her pocket, Biddy stood up and
started to dust the furniture. She never sat for any length of time;
and even though she kept herself busy, I never felt that she was
distracted by attending to other tasks while we talked. Early on in
our relationship, I began to feel at ease with her bustling about. It
was just a part of who she was. While continuing to dust, she said:

> I heard some time ago that during wartime
> shortages, often, the only available lines were
> the party lines. All in all, the idea worked well
> at the time, but there were shortfalls like with
> anything.

I quipped, "Such as?"

> Well, especially disturbing was that — if
> someone was on their phone and someone else
> on the party line picked theirs up to use, you
> could get in the way of when that person
> wanted to talk. If your party line was shared
> with a real gas bag, you might be obliged to
> wait a long time to make your call. Some gas

bags would take a long time to get all their gas
out, you know.

Then, there would be those nosey nellies that
would sneak in on a call, where they could hear
the already ongoing conversation. There were
some pretty sordid stories spread and a whole
heap of marriages split up due to the
eavesdropping, I can assure you. Probably,
went so far as blackmail and even murder!

My curiosity was really at a peak when I said, "No! Really? You
think?" Biddy answered:

Sure. Think about it. You pick up the phone
to call good ol' Uncle Gustoff and you find
yourself smack dab in the middle of a
conversation that includes a plot to rob a bank.
The bad guys don't know you're listening. You
get all the information you need for a good
game of blackmail. You contact the parties
involved, and let 'em know your intentions.

I asked, "You know, Biddy, I had not considered that. So, what
about the murder?" Her response, "What about it?" I replied, "Well,
you said blackmail and even murder." She chuckled, "Yes, I did, O.
Don't tell me you didn't think that blackmailing is a no-consequence
crime, did ya?" At this, Biddy regained focus:

There I go, getting off the track, again! These
blasted new devices, the phone especially —
just too complicated — don't even know why
they call 'em phones anymore. They do just
about everything, exceptin' cleaning your teeth,
and rarely do folks even talk on 'em. They do
that sexting thing. God forbid, anyone should
have a conversation that involves two people
taking turns talking to each other!

I hesitated, "I think you've got the sexting and texting mixed up,
Biddy." She quipped, "What's that?" I answered:

> You said, 'they do that sexting thing.' I think
> you mean, *texting* — that people don't talk to
> each other that much anymore — they text
> each other instead.

"Now, wait a minute," Biddy put the dusting cloth down on the table
next to her, and she sat back down:

> Don't people sext on these new-fangled
> phones? Share pictures of their 'junk,' I think
> they call it. Heard all kinds of names for
> people's parts over the years. Heard 'em called
> 'our business' or 'our privates.' Some people
> actually name their 'parts' — maybe, a Willie or
> a Lilly Lou — never 'our junk.' I've heard so
> many names over the years. Some were pretty
> awful and some, well, I couldn't help but laugh
> when I heard 'em.

Curious with what she would come up with next, I interrupted,
"Okay, Biddy, you've got to share some of them with me." Biddy
chimed in:

> Ok now, let me think. And, as a side note —
> just this morning, Ernst said to me, 'I've got to
> think for a minute,' and I said back to him, 'If
> you must dear, but I wouldn't waste my time.'
> We got a kick out of that. Funny how we
> *olders* — that's what I call us — find humor in
> most everything. Some would think it's quaint.
> Some'd be sure we were nuts. I like to think,
> we're just us.
>
> Young folks are way too serious. We were too,
> back then, I suppose. If they would just listen
> to us now, though, how different their lives
> could be. Guess that's what the 'olders' have
> been chanting through the ages. I think, if just
> one generation of the 'youngers' did listen, what
> a different place we'd all be in. It's all a waste
> of time to worry 'bout most stuff, like getting

old or not livin' long enough to gettin' there.
Either way, waste of time. I live by the one 'T'
and two 'R's' rule.

Venturing out at this point, I asked, "What does that mean, the
two R's and one T?"

Biddy instantly responded:

This is it. Right now. Right here! Anyway,
back to all the different names — not trying to
be 'politically correct.' By the way, I always
thought that saying was as stupid as stupid gets.
Politically correct. HA!

But, I'm drifting again — where was I? Oh yes,
names for the man's 'hangin' dangly' or the
term more acceptable in the scientific
community, 'the penile member.' There's the
'meat whistle.' And here's a good one, the 'one-
eyed trouser worm'! My mother called the
woman's 'genitalia.' Now there's a word —
Genitalia. Say it over and over again, O.

I replied politely, "Thank you, no."

Genitalia, genitalia, genitalia! Depending
on where you put the emphasis, it could very
well sound like a woman's name. Don't ya
think, O? 'Genitalia, would you be so kind to
meet me in the vestibule so we may adjourn to
the garden for tea?' NO! YIKES!

Biddy's raised voice startled me and sent chills down my arms and
legs.

"What is it, Biddy?" I had no idea what had so suddenly crossed her
mind, and as I managed to get the question out of my mouth, she
had already managed to answer:

A woman's vestibule is the area surrounding
her vagina. Now, there we go with another

one — Vagina, vagina, vagina!

Ernst was nowhere to be seen, but we heard him ask in a somewhat
hesitant voice, "You girls aren't playing Pin-The-Tail-On-The-
Donkey, are you?"

"Not yet dear." Biddy quickly answered and then continued:

Anyway, for those that would know the
'vestibule,' it is the area, as I said, surrounding
the you know what . . . . That sample sentence,
I used, could be considered pretty racy in
certain circles of people. Still though, it doesn't
have the same impact as 'genitalia,' or what my
mother called the 'woman's genitalia' — getting
back to my thought — She called it 'their
business.'

"She called it *their business*?" My face scrunched as I asked Biddy, and
she answered:

Yes ma'am, she sure did. Imagine my
confusion when I heard more women were
opening up their own businesses all over the
country! Downright disgusting, I thought.

Pictures of their junk? One-eyed trouser worms? And, Lord help
me, meat whistles? How did she know these terms? And where did
Lily Lou come from? I was sure this was more information than I
needed to know; and I suppose my face showed it, because Biddy
immediately clarified that she was not referring to her and Ernst —
of course:

"Don't you fret now, O, junk to us is still just stuff we throw away."

*****

I hear folks share their pictures with everyone
and their mothers now, and they're typing sex
talk to each other. Guess that's foreplay today.
No more working your way around the bases.

> Wham bam, and it's a home run! Hell, takes
> half the fun outta it, if ya ask me.

Biddy took a long look out of the window saying nothing more for a few, very quiet moments. Then, adjusting herself in her chair again, she took a slow, deep breath and exhaled before continuing:

> Gettin' there, really is half the fun. Yes, I do
> remember that. Couldn't remember if I put my
> teeth in today, but I remember that. Ah, to be
> young and impetuous.

> The boys trying to find the hooks on the girls'
> brassieres! Now that was a hoot, I tell ya. And
> all that kissin' and touchin'. Seems a shame,
> some of the time it'd be over — before it got
> started! — still, not as much a shame as leaving
> all that part out to start with.

She shook her head from side to side and proceeded with:

> Tsk, tsk, tsk — They send this junk, no pun
> intended, with these new phones. The phones
> that have cameras, flashlights — even adding
> machines and everything one can imagine in
> 'em, right?

She had me there. There are those who do *just that* with their phones, and I quickly responded, "Yes, some do exactly that." Biddy responded:

> Well now, a phone is for talking into — not
> picture taking and all the other malarkey they
> do now-a-days. Can't complain, really. I've
> taken a picture or two on mine — once I
> figured out how! Actually, I wanted to send
> Ernst a picture of my nipples.

She tilted her head to the side and gave me a wink. By this time, I had learned to sit with my hand just under my jaw. This way, I could hold my chin up on those occasions when it started to drop open, like when she stated:

> Let me tell ya, gettin' 'em up high enough to get
> a good shot from underneath where the little
> darlings live now-a-days was one hell of a
> project. Started out steppin' up on a chair 'till I
> figured out, that just raised all of me. Damn
> nipples were still too low to get the blasted
> camera in the right place to get the shot I
> wanted!

I waited for her to laugh, feeling certain she would. Instead, she went on, quite seriously:

> A few shots ended up being of my knees, one
> of the chair, and another couple were of just
> the tips of my shoes — oh, and several of my
> own thumb.

> Gotta tell ya, O, I even tried lying flat on my
> back to get a good picture of the elusive devils.
> Thought I was pretty alluring in one. That is,
> 'till my breasts slid off my chest and up and
> over my shoulders. Got so I was just out of
> patience and frustrated, so I handed him the
> phone and said I'd done somethin' special for
> only his eyes.

> Nope, I got less than no patience, you know.
> Just handed him the phone — all at my wit's
> end. You know, those pictures never seemed
> to get him going. He never comments on 'em.
> Only asks me why I took pictures of the tips of
> my shoes. Should of got his help, I guess, me
> with having no patience and all.

I speculated, asking, "And your Ernst has the patience it takes, I'm assuming."

> That he does. Look, O, our being married —
> even more — *his being married to me* all these
> years didn't just happen. We had to have a
> gimmick — one that would work for *him*.

Interesting, I thought, "What would that gimmick have been, Biddy?"
She replied:

> Simple — patience — yup, patience for him
> and stirring up those embers now and again for
> me. You know, O, sometimes I think my
> embers are just a flint away from an explosion.

After a long pause, Biddy got up and waved for me to follow her into
the kitchen. I started to adjust myself in the chair, I chose to sit in at
the table; and Biddy started talking, just as I pushed the Record
button. After retrieving one bag of asparagus and another bag
containing mushrooms from the refrigerator, she washed the
contents of both bags and left them to drain in the colander which
she had placed in the sink. Next to the sink, the counter was lined
with fresh tomatoes; she gathered several in her arms, then took
them to the colander and gently set them on top — running water
over everything.

I marveled at how Biddy made food preparation look so easy. It
wasn't just cooking. She made a lot of things seem that way — a
talent, I had started to envy early on in our relationship.

Cooking to me seemed like such a chore. It wasn't that I did not like
to cook. There were times when I really did enjoy it. Most often,
though, cooking seemed like it was just a means to an end. This was
not true for Biddy, no. She could cook a meal, carry on a
conversation, feed and water her many plants, talk on the telephone
and attend to any number of her other "chores" — the whole time,
making it all look like second nature to her — no effort
accompanying any of it.

Once, she told me:

> You make it way too hard, O. You're thinking
> about all you've got to do. That *makes* it hard.
> I just do it and think about everything else!
> And, there is always something else to think
> about.

Biddy grabbed the hand towel to dry her hands, and while looking out the window above the kitchen sink, she startled me by saying, "Back to your question about this election, O — "

I had all but forgotten that I had even asked Biddy the question — what, with all the territory we had covered, since I had first asked her about it earlier in the day. She started with:

> Let me tell you, O, I've seen and heard many a politician over my lifetime. It gets to the point where they all seem to meld into one — one big, fat cat after another telling hippo-sized piles of lies.
>
> I think they come from a place where they mean well in the beginning. Somehow, though, they get caught up in themselves and how big they feel. We're just the little people. And, while they're being driven around in fancy cars (paid for by the little people) and eating in marble-walled cafeterias at the White House — the 'people's house,' mind you — the little people are packing what food they can afford to buy into brown bags for their kids' lunches.
>
> Don't get me wrong. There've been a few that did their danged best to keep their promises, but the other folks — the ones from another party — wouldn't let 'em. Stopped 'em at every turn. Sometimes, I think, just 'cause they could — you know, being mean-spirited, spiteful, like spoiled brats and weak-minded bullies. And, they all do it. One side will point their shaky finger at the other, but they're all guilty of it. All of 'em. Plenty unfair, and downright wrong if ya ask me.

I acquiesced:

> Yes, I agree. Seems like we never let whoever is in office to try out their ideas completely. It's like they got voted in because the majority

wanted them in, but once there, well, no one
wants to work with *them*. It's unfair.

Biddy barked back:

> Unfair? Hell, it sure is, to us! Damn time they
> do their damn jobs. And that job is to help
> *ALL* the people. To do that, they'd have to
> compromise, wouldn't they?

I nodded in affirmation, "Absolutely, I agree." And, I did agree.
Even if I had not agreed, I would not admit to it *now*! Clearly angry
now, Biddy said:

> Yes, compromise. Maybe they don't know the
> meaning of the word — kind of surprising
> since most of 'em have been to college and all.
> Compromise, you give up a little and so does
> the other side. That way, both sides get some
> of what they want — better than no one gettin'
> *anything* they want.

> I tell ya, O, I'd like to take the whole bunch of
> 'em out to the wood shed. 'Either get your act
> together, or get your act out a here,' is what I
> would say to 'em. Move your fat 'n lazy asses
> right on back to where ya come from.

Her voice had reached a pitch, I had not heard before.

> They think they're some kind a royalty. Hate to
> tell ya folks you're not in England — no kings
> and queens here. You're elected officials, damn
> it. You're not our bosses, we're YOURS!

She had started cutting the tomatoes into chunks and added them to
the mixture of asparagus pieces and sliced mushrooms which she had
placed onto an aluminum foil-lined cookie sheet. I feared she would
chop off the tip of her finger, but I was even more wary to interrupt
her and advise her to be careful.

Her voice — an octave or two higher than a few moments before —
clearly on a rant, she fumed:

> Remember the folks that put you there. The
> ones that are paying your wages now and will
> be paying for your insurance and retirement for
> the rest of your snifflin', whiny assess life!
> Now, do your damn jobs or take your greedy,
> grimy-lying asses back to where they come
> from!

I jumped in my chair, when I heard the backdoor close and saw
Ernst standing in the hallway.

> Biddy, I can hear you all the way into the
> backyard. Now you're going to scare poor
> O — not to mention the citizenry in the next
> town, down the island.

Ernst's tone of voice, too, had risen.

Biddy swung her head around and, for a quick second, gave Ernst a
look which I would rather no one ever give to me. Then, just as
quickly, I heard her say, "O will be just fine. And, couldn't your shop
do with some straightening?"

Ernst's voice, now slightly softer, queried, "Biddy?"

With her eyebrows raised slightly, her tone of voice still stern
(although somewhat gentler); she looked directly into his eyes,
"*Ernst?*"

And there it was. Although, not the kind she had spoken of
earlier — I had seen and felt the embers *and patience*. Yes, I had felt
the patience too.

As I gathered my things that night to leave, Biddy had me write down
the recipe on how to bake her asparagus-mushroom-tomato-garlic-
and-pepper dish. When done, she said that she would scoop it over
hot, brown rice and sprinkle the works with Parmesan cheese. There
was to be no more discussion of politics, and this was a good place to
end what had, indeed, been a long day.

Heading down their front stairs, I turned to wave another "goodbye,"
when I saw through the window that they were swaying in a loving
embrace. That is when I more clearly realized that Biddy and Ernst

preferred to place more importance on their relationship than on their opinions. This was something that differentiated them from the 'youngers' (as Biddy liked to call anyone not receiving retirement benefits).

Not more than thirty minutes had passed before I left, when Biddy was, in her own words, "mad as a wet hen." Ernst, firm in his tone when he addressed her, still carried in his words, a "glimmer of humor," helping to ease the situation. Her anger was quietly calmed. That which made her so angry quickly lost its importance. In its place, they chose their priorities. Now, they were holding each other. As I made my way down to the car, I could hear them laughing.

Biddy had made this comment some time before:

> Don't let anything stand in the way of showing
> your love to those for whom you feel it. This
> life is far too short to waste time, only to
> discover this truth too close to the end of it.

She had reiterated how she wished that just one generation of 'youngers' would listen to the 'olders' — for she believed if they did, humankind would be much better off for that generation, if not for others'.

*****

As I entered our house, I saw the kids sitting around the coffee table. The boys were noisily playing a video game with the volume turned up to an agitating level. Bella was trying to draw a picture of what looked like a unicorn. Her brother, Jake, kept putting his foot a couple of inches away from her picture, and Bella would immediately push it away. At that point, he would annoyingly put it right back.

Mike was getting a bowl out of the refrigerator and called out to me, "Hey Babe, are you hungry? I found some leftover spaghetti and can heat it up while you take a shower, if you like."

I entered the kitchen and whispered in his ear, "I would rather you join me."

"*Eww gross, mom!*" Allen yelled out. If only his hearing was as acute as when he was told to put his dirty underwear in the hamper or to take his finger out of his nose.

> Mommy, Jake won't stop putting his stinky foot
> on my picture. Stop it, Jake. Mommy, he's
> putting it in my face. *STOP IT — MOMMY!*

After this rant, I ordered:

> Jake, get your foot out of your sister's face right
> now, and turn that game off! Both you and
> your brother — get to your homework. Bella,
> get ready for your bath. Dad and I will make
> dinner, and if baths and homework are all done
> by the time it's ready, *MAYBE*, just *MAYBE*, I
> will make hot-fudge sundaes for desert.

"Why'd ya say, maybe?" Jake piped up as he put one foot on his sister's picture and the other — still covered with a dirty sock — right up to her face.

Bella blurted out while swinging her arm madly at her brother, "Mommy! He did it again!"

She did not need to tell me. It was something I expected, as it was a typical act on his part to get in one last, parting shot. I was all too familiar with the fact that there was always at least one in the group — especially, my group.

> Because, *MAYBE* I will, and *MAYBE* I won't.
> Depends on your attitudes, and if I have to tell
> you again to get to your homework
> and baths —

With that, I looked directly at all three of them and finished with:

> I'll add extra walnuts and let you add the
> whipped cream to your own sundae if you do it
> now. Oh, and this is a group effort. If any one
> of you does not do what you're told — not a
> one of you gets desert. Now get to it!

Surprisingly, they all headed in the directions they needed to. Not one said a thing about the fairness or unfairness of my "group effort" comment either. Instead, they all started in with their respective assignments.

Mike looked up at me with a cute grin, "Good on ya, ma!" he chuckled.

I replied, "Don't expect it to work all the time," as I put my arms around his neck.

Holding onto Mike and knowing how deeply we loved each other, I recognized that lately, neither one of us had taken the time to tell each other just how much we did. I could not help but wonder how different our lives may be if I was to heed Biddy's advice. I heard her voice resonate in my ears:

> Don't let anything stand in the way of showing
> your love to those for whom you feel it. This
> life is far too short to waste time, only to
> discover this truth too close to the end of it.

Seeing Biddy and Ernst together earlier and, now, being in the arms of the man I loved: I did not doubt that my heeding Biddy's advice would be well worth my time.

Chapter 9

SITTIN' PRETTY

In some instances, time seems to stand still. In others, time flies by way too fast. I have found, like most everyone does, this is true when it comes to doing something enjoyable.

Looking back on that first year I spent with Biddy, I realized it wasn't just that I had grown to love both she and Ernst — there was more to it.

Up to the point of first meeting Ernst and Biddy, my life could be compared with my having been away from home for a long time. After getting to know both of them, that comparison changed to my feeling like I had returned home and was being welcomed by old friends.

Somehow, in the midst of my ordinary life, I happened to find this woman. As I learned more about Biddy's life and those people she shared it with, I knew that if I never met any of the characters she referred to, I would come to know them through her colorful stories.

Some of the people mentioned in Biddy's stories had a good soul and were caring people. I found myself growing fond of so many of them. Others were of questionable character, to say the least. I felt repugnance towards some and hostility towards others; and with some, I felt a strong, positive emotional connection.

In light of all this drama, Biddy would laugh. She got quite a kick out of my candid (and mostly naïve) responses to the "immense gathering of her life's sidekicks," as she liked to call them. As she paraded her characters and their stories before me, their lives' circumstances unfolded: some were deeply serious; others left me laughing hysterically, and none were nondescript.

While gathering information for our book and learning about Biddy and Ernst's relationship from listening to the stories — that deep well of stories — I was also introduced to a new part of myself, a part of me that was foreign and unfamiliar. It was a part, though, that I had become increasingly comfortable with.

My "new self" was fun, likable and even interesting. Most of all, my newly found self did not need so much reassurance from the outer world. And, although it took me a considerable amount of time, I was readjusting to being okay with just being me. That was the part I liked the most.

In the beginning of our relationship, Biddy had said that I needed to come out of my shell more often. My gut response, while trying to be funny, was that I was "not a turtle."

When I relayed this exchange to Mike, he asked, "What was her reply?" I answered him honestly, "Brisk — her response was brisk, very brisk."

"Then don't act like one," she yelled. "And for God sakes, come out snapping. That beak's for more than just tearing up lettuce!" — classic Biddy.

We had been thorough when it came to going through drawers, boxes and even an old satchel or two, which contained squashed up scraps of paper with "Biddy scribbles," as I called them. Even with all our efforts considered, we barely scratched the surface of the abundance of information they held.

Often, Biddy would find a note and then start to tell the story that related directly to it — something that always amazed me, as some notes were decades old. Off she would go — she would travel to that place always leaving me to wonder where it would lead us. Without a doubt, though, there would be another story or, more often than not, a few stories that would follow.

I had lost the "interviewer" position somewhere in the very beginning of our venture. I felt okay about it, though, for all I had really wanted to do was to collect whatever she would offer.

Late into the night when everyone was sleeping, and then again, early in the morning while riding the Old 32, I would listen to the tapes and review my notes. With every bit of my brain power, I would start to build on the body of information for our book. Looking back, this was an exciting and challenging time in my life.

Contemplating the order in which I would have to put all this information together into one book, was a task I had tried to keep at bay. I would listen, read, write and repeat all of that over and over again. Processing the information, including my thoughts about it, led me to think that it would all eventually fall into place — hopefully. My newest mantra had become one like that of Scarlett O' Hare in *Gone with The Wind*: I would worry about that tomorrow. After all, tomorrow was another day.

*****

Tomorrow came sooner than I had expected. I realized that organizing was the biggest hurdle I had to overcome — and overcome it, I must. There was never a shortage of stories. There were, in fact, hundreds of them. Given the chance, an experienced writer could write hundreds of books from just the notes Biddy had stored in an old checkbook box which she had kept in her kitchen "junk drawer."

And so, I thought, what would Biddy do? On occasion, she may have appeared to be a little off center — scattered — if you will. In actuality, though, she was usually very much on top of everything in her life. Pondering that subject, I reflected on a time during one of our sessions.

We had reached a lull in the conversation, and Biddy seemed to be getting tired when she looked at the pile of notes on the sun room table and said, "No way to do it, 'ceptin' to dive right in." At that point, she stuck her hand into the pile and grabbed a note:

> Okay then. This one was to remind me of the guy that didn't want to change his seating on the plane. So, this deadbeat — I'll call him Ken, or better, Sittin' Pretty — yeah. So, Sittin' Pretty says to me:
>
>> 'Biddy, *the wife* respects your advice. It's beyond me as to

why. But since she's not
speaking to me right now, I
thought I'd reach out to you for
whatever *rich* advice you can
come up with.'

He goes on to say:

'We, mostly, *the wife,* decided to
plan a vacation with another
couple this year. Lucky me.
This couple she wants to take
this trip with are not in my
financial circle, if you get where
I'm coming from. I know this
because they have to fly
Economy.'

'I, on the other hand, can afford
to fly First-Class and told *the
wife,* I plan to do just that. If
she wants to sit back in
Economy with our friends
instead of with me in First-
Class, let her get leg cramps.
I'm going to purchase my First-
Class ticket, whether or not she
sits next to me. What do you
think about that?'

Well now, let me see. *The wife?* I suppose
you're referring to your wife? You didn't say,
and I had a hard time catchin' any personal
connection there. I kinda doubt my advice will
be *rich* enough for your blood, Ken. Be assured
though, I get where you are coming from. My
biggest concern is where you are headin' . . . .

Tell ya this Ken, sounds like you should get any
ticket that you like that suits your needs —
maybe one that seats you as far away from

anyone else as possible. I'd advise you to
consider travelin' to a different continent, too,
than with *the wife* — whether she be your's or
someone else's.

Ya see, Ken, you sound like you're about as
much fun a travelin' companion as a burstin'
butt boil! Happy travels!

I remembered sitting back in my chair and saying, "You know, Biddy,
sounds like you should have suggested he take a trip to see a place
that had a 'pile of sumpin'.'"

At that, she smacked her leg and screeched, "That's my girl, O! Now
you're gettin' it!"

Remembering that "incident" during our session gave me the answer
I needed as to "how to organize" our book.

Just *dive right in.*

Chapter 10

SITTIN' TOO LONG

Introducing Biddy would be easy. Describing the angles of her persona would not be terribly difficult. However, describing her inner self — better yet, *her selves* — would require, a simple mortal such as I, more deep concentration.

I learned early on in our relationship that Biddy was more of a complex individual than my simple introduction of her would allow. But, then again, I found this to be true of everyone I encountered. While people may appear to me to be as one way on the outside (for example, like artichokes), there actually exists on the inside many layers to an individual. This acknowledgment was no less true in my observance of Biddy and, as I was discovering, no less true for me, too.

I had reached a juncture, where I felt I was facing quite a dilemma. Biddy would have said that I found myself "in a pickle." Either way, I struggled with my dilemma of deciding which story I should start with. There were so many I liked. I felt like this was an impossible assignment — to pick a favorite. Soon, however, I concluded the problem was not about picking favorites.

Although not every story contained advice (even if that was the original intent of the book), every one of them had something of a life's lesson in it. Then, there were those stories, I swear, Biddy told just to see what kind of reaction she could get from me. Some stories were to test my alertness, if you will. She enjoyed leading me down the rabbit hole — a hole I ventured down more often than not. With my eyes wide open and innocently naïve, I merrily followed her. So often, I found, she had led me there only for a bit of fun.

Then suddenly, unexpectedly, I had an epiphany. Biddy had said, "We'll do it like a conversation." Yes, now I remembered her saying that. I decided to write in a style likened to replicating people engaging one another in casual conversation.

And so, I began with a conversation Biddy and I had sometime during that first year. It did not matter at which point it had started — one, three or eight months into our relationship — like so much of our time spent together, organization of time was irrelevant. My epiphany opened my eyes to the fact, that *when* something was said did not matter so much as *what* was said.

*****

While I was writing the beginning of the book, I recognized that the relationship between Biddy and her stories were much like that of best, lifelong friends. They may not have spoken for years but when they did, oh boy!

The feelings evoked in Biddy when telling one of her stories were akin to those of children in the hot-summer sun jumping off of the dock into their favorite, summer lake. At first, they would be breathless when hitting the cold water; but as they sank deeper, before popping back up to the surface, they would be hypnotically engulfed in the pleasure of it.

That is like what Biddy's stories were to her — lifelong friends. They made her feel just like those kids jumping into the lake. And, just like old friends that have not spoken in decades, once she started telling them — *oh boy*!

The particular conversation I am referring to did not start like most of them with her saying, "Okay, O, here's another one," as she would take out another piece of old scratch paper with her Biddy scribbles on it. This one started on a Saturday after Ernst, Mike and the kids had gone to the beach. Biddy was trying to decide what to fix for lunch and came across an over-ripe cantaloupe sitting on her counter.

"Nobody asked for this advice, but sure as hell that's never stopped me before," she exhaled heavily with a chuckle:

> Had to renew my driver's license awhile back.
> Always thought that was just a whole lot of

hoopla. I've been driving since before I named 'dirt'! No reason, as I can see, to renew this or that anymore. Hell, I ain't killed myself or nobody else. Takin' that into account, seems I'm a damn, good driver or just sneaky enough to avoid troubles. Either way, leave well enough alone, I say.

And, oh Lordy, O, how I hate going to those places. Was going to do it on the computer. Learned enough about that damn-founded thing, I can do at least that much on one. As hard as the geniuses make it, applying for anything on the computer now-a-days — mix that with 'it's a government site' — Lord help us all. You know, O, between you and me, it would be a whole lot simpler if they'd given the job to a smart person to design the blasted website instead of some wet-behind-the-ears college graduate. You know the type, I'm sure. *Uppity pecker-woods!* Think they got it all figured out and can do anything better than anybody else. Hand 'em a shovel and they'd probably knock themselves out with it trying to figure which end goes where. I'd like to show a couple of 'em where I'd like to put it!

I cleared my throat, not that I needed to, only in the hopes it would distract Biddy just long enough for her to get back to her story before "working herself up into a froth," as Ernst would say. Even though he was not there at the time, I could hear him in my mind saying, "Now Biddy."

It seemed to help to some extent, but not before she added:

Hell, learnin' all I've had to in my lifetime — ya know, O — all that stuff is doing more than holding the sides of my head from caving in. Ya'd never know it with the way those degree-toting, or just plain, smart-ass youngers treat us

olders. Far as I'm concerned, figuring out these
damn sites is a hell of an accomplishment.

So, now I got myself all settled in on their site,
and this warning of sorts pops up in all this red
writing, tellin' me I had to go to my local office.
I thought, hell, why? I'd done it using the
computer the last time. But the 'alert' message
kept saying I had to go in this time.

To tell ya the truth, O, I think it was just 'cuz of
my age. Somebody down there just wanted to
see the face of a gal with a birth date as old as
mine! Not too many fun perks working for the
government, I guess.

Biddy took a quick glance at me over her rhinestone-reading age-
paraphernalia interjecting, "No offense intended, O."

My response, "None taken." Then in a ceremonious fashion, I
waved my hand encouraging her to continue.

"So anyway, in a bit of a snit, I tell Ernst to get ready, 'we're going for
a ride,' and I load him up in the car." Going forward in a bit of a
huff, Biddy said:

I really hate those places, O. Used to hate the
Social Security place too, 'till I met you!
Anyhow, I stood in line for quite a spell and
that was just waitin' to pull my number, and the
place was packed. Knew for sure, it was going
to be a long wait. Was glad I remembered to
crack the window open for Ernst. He fell
asleep on the way over there. Ridin' in the car
does that to him. I didn't see no cause to wake
him.

At that point, I remembered it had come to my attention over time
that Biddy could and would speak differently depending on the
occasion, time and/or subject matter. One sentence would come out
of her as if she were an old-school English teacher. Clearly, one
could see this was where the usage and propriety of her words were

taken into the utmost consideration. Yet, as early as the next sentence, her words would tumble out of her mouth as if an uneducated, old-dirt farmer had said them. There were many times when, upon completing a sentence, I would half expect her to spit out chew.

I had never really wanted to pin down the cause of these behaviors. It made me happy just to be with either of these Biddy characters as well as with any of her other characters I had come to know. With that in mind, Biddy carried on:

> There were all kinds of folks standin' 'round,
> but I didn't want to do that anymore. I found
> an open seat 'tween a man that started coughin'
> and a gaggin' like he had a fair-sized hair ball
> getting ready to be up-chucked, while he was
> wiping his runny nose with the sleeve of his oil-
> stained shirt and a woman — God help me —
> I can only describe as a mouth-breather. If I
> weren't so damn tired from drivin' all the way
> down there and standin' in line so long, I'd a
> gotten the hell out a there. Gone home and
> jumped right in the bathtub.
>
> Finally, after a really, very long time I heard my
> number called. It was kinda a long shot, I
> would hear anything else with all the hackin'
> and a huein' and heavy breathin' going on, not
> to mention the smells. But then I just did,
> didn't I! Felt like my skin had stuff crawlin' all
> over it. Know what I mean? Anything ever
> make ya feel like that? Like you're in some
> kinda science experiment.

I responded honestly, "Unfortunately, Biddy, I can relate. I've been in many — and I do mean *many* and more than I care to remember — similar situations."

"Oh yes, of course you have dear." She was quick to say, "at your work place." I responded:

Well, yeah. I would like to say, 'only there,' but
no, on the way to work too. Oh, and lest I
forget, just going to the grocery store is an
experience. There, I'm exposed to people
coughing, gagging and expelling any number of
bodily fluids. So much so, I have nearly thrown
up on any number of them!

I could see that my candid response caused Biddy to blink with
surprise. She gasped, "Oh, O. You must find another line of work!"
I answered, "You've got that right, Biddy. And I'm working on it!"

At that, we turned to each other, and for that briefest of seconds, our
eyes spoke to and were understood by each other. And then, Biddy
responded with, "My yes, O, indeed you are."

"Now, let's see. Where was I?" Biddy looked up at the ceiling for a
moment, and then with an affirmative nod of her head, she opened
with:

> Tell ya, O, for an old broad, I was up darn
> fast — as fast as this old Biddy can be after
> sittin' too long. It takes a bit more to get the
> blood flowin' down there anymore. Used to be
> my butt was firm, and up here.

Biddy gestured to where she believed her butt used to be, "Not down
to the back of the knees where it lives now!" And, as what had
become a frequent and most enjoyable event we had come to share,
our laughter ensued.

> Made my way to a nice enough young fella that
> got me all set up — after doing what I had to
> do with lookin' in that eye-piece set-up to see if
> I was still able to see whatever the hell it was I
> was supposed to be lookin' at! Don't get it
> really. Why don't they have pictures of stop
> signs or kids chasing balls out into the street?
> Maybe, a chunk a some road kill now and again.
> The kinda things ya see when ya driving and
> those things you try to miss hittin' — instead of
> blinking lights and letters and whatever the hell

else was in that stupid little black box.
Confounded confusing, I say. We argued a
little bit 'bout what I was supposed to be
seeing. He said one thing. I said 'hell no!' This
went on until he said he couldn't take it
anymore, stamped my paper and said I passed.
That's when I stepped down off the steppin'
stool he'd lent me, so as I could get up to the
blasted thing. Anyway, after all of this, I
thought this nice young fella and I was back on
good terms, until he asks me if I want to donate
my organs! Can ya believe it, O?

I nodded my head up and down as I, too, was asked that when I went in to get my license. I said to her, "Yes, Biddy, they ask everyone that."

"Well," Biddy scoffed, "I said, 'Not 'til Hell freezes or 'till I'm done using 'em, sonny boy!'"

Biddy's sense of righteousness was truly something to admire. I know, I had begun to do so.

At this point, Biddy opened her kitchen garbage can and tossed the over-ripe cantaloupe into it. When it hit the bottom of the can, it made a very loud (and in unison) thump-and-splat sound.

That is when she turned to me and said in a very matter-of-fact monotone voice:

Old Biddy butts that sit too long are much like
cantaloupes restin' on a counter. If you don't
turn 'em now and again, they get all soft 'n
squishy.

Today's advice, O? Turn your fruit!

Chapter 11

AND THE LIST GOES ON

Compiling all of my notes and listening to all of my recordings over and over, not leaving anything out, took me a great deal of time. I had to take a step back to see just how far I had gone, how many chapters were included in Biddy's book and how much it had grown. When I completed this endeavor, I found that her memoirs were more extensive than I had expected, and there was still more to add! Giving much thought to my predicament, I decided: That which was so hard to start was now going to be as equally hard to end.

Knowing that I did not want to leave anything important out of Biddy's book, I concluded that I had to pick a cut-off point, or the number of pages her book would entail could be equal to those of the classic, written works of Tolstoy's *War and Peace*.

This enduring process, however, did give me an idea — what if we did a series of books? That would be great, I thought, sure — a series of Biddy's books! Now, I wondered, what would she think of that idea? I would keep my idea on the back-burner and wait for a better time to offer her my suggestion.

Biddy had more stories, even if she had to make them up. I suspected that she had done so on more than one occasion. I had no doubt that she would ever run out of material; either way, I was always interested and intrigued to hear more of her stories.
I thought, of course, her audience would be interested, too, which led me to remember one of her wilder stories about a bet between her and Ernst.

Biddy and I had taken a quick trip to the grocery store to pick up some goodies for the kids. At the entrance to the parking lot, we saw a panhandler holding a cardboard sign on which he had scribbled,

"Lost job. Will work for food." Upon seeing this, Biddy instructed me to stop, and she started rummaging through her satchel. I turned to look at her to see if she was serious. This was neither a good place to stop nor was it a good time for Biddy to be in one of her "let's-mess-with-O," moods.

Biddy turned her head towards me and said, "I'm damn serious, O, like a heart-attack serious. Stop the car!" With a hard swallow and a push on the brake, I did just as she said.

The man, who had dirty hair and clothes and quite obviously more than a day's worth of beard growth, came to her window as she rolled it down. I quickly contemplated whether I should get ready to hit the gas or lock the doors. I poised one foot over the gas pedal while holding the other firm on the brake. My hands were tightly held around the steering wheel, and I could feel my heart begin to beat harder.

Biddy pulled something out of her satchel — a folded piece of paper — and I thought, "Oh God, please don't be an advice note!" He took the paper she handed to him, and then she instructed, "Now, you call this number and ask for Jack."

My mind raced. What was the punch line going to be? I felt my hands sweating on the steering wheel, while I tried to somehow prepare myself for what horrible, awkward event was going to follow. Would Biddy dare to say, "Call and ask for Jack — Jack Ass, ya bum, go get a job!" — or something equally as bad, or even worse. Instead, she said:

> Jack is a friend of mine and needs some work
> done on his barn. He's a good man. There's a
> phone in the grocery store in the pharmacy
> department. Ask for Patty. Tell her Biddy sent
> ya. She'll let you use the phone to call him.
> Better do it right away 'cuz he won't wait
> around, and he'll find someone else real quick.
> He'll pay ya well and maybe even let ya stay a
> day or two while ya do the work.

I did not know exactly what had just happened. It all seemed completely legitimate on Biddy's part. Understandably, it had taken me some time to develop the habit of my "waiting for the other shoe to drop." I was just not sure if this was one of those times. The panhandler took the piece of paper, opened it and bent down to Biddy's window and said, "Bless you ma'am. Bless you. I will call him now." I could see his eyes had the beginning of joy-tears welling up in them.

My heart felt like that of the Grinch in a Dr. Seuss storybook. I swear, I could feel my heart growing. What a kind gesture Biddy had displayed. She touched this man's life in such a positive way, it was all I could do to not shed a tear myself — what a moment. And that is exactly what it ended up being — just a moment.

Suddenly, we heard a loud horn honking in back of us, to which Biddy's immediate response was to wildly wave her right hand out of her window, her middle finger pronounced and erect. Whatever she was yelling evades me now. In my startled condition, I forgot I had one foot on the brake and the other on the accelerator. This oversight and lapse in memory caused us to lurched forward and then backwards. Being in the flustered and confused state I was in, I had mistaken the gear I was in and accelerated right after putting the car in reverse.

*****

Constance Birdsboro just so happened to be the proud owner of a brand-new, bright-red Mercedes Benz. She ranted breathlessly over and over again, about how her car had barely a hundred miles on it. My ten-year-old car, also a foreign number — a faded blue Civic to be precise — had more than one-hundred-thousand miles on it. Although I could have boasted about this fact, I decided it was not a necessity at that juncture.

The unfortunate combination of my mentally challenged condition, at the time, resulted in my knee-jerk reaction while in the wrong gear. This caused my Civic to break the headlights and yank a good portion loose of Constance Birdsboro's front grill. An additional result of this temporary brain blip was the extraordinary fashion in which both our bumpers were compressed into one another — what was left of them.

While the three of us, Constance Birdsboro, Biddy and I, waited for the police to arrive, two men approached us. One was a heavy-set, unshaven fellow whose odor could only be described as that of death in a rotting cabbage patch. The other man was taller and less dapper than the first man. This second man's odor could easily be mistaken for that of an oil can being used as an ashtray. The metal screw going through his eyebrow and another one on the left side of his nose, as well as the big silver rings through both his earlobes, made it difficult for me to keep eye contact with him.

These two men were amiable enough and offered me the name of a guy who knew a guy who knew someone else of whom such man had some kind of connection to a body shop. They could do the work on both my ten-year-old Civic and Constance Birdsboro's brand-new, bright-red Mercedes Benz with less than a hundred miles on it — a fact Constance Birdsboro would repeat to the point of exhaustion. They said we could save a lot of money by going this route — maybe even getting all the work done for about half as much as it would cost to take our cars to a better known and, perhaps, more reputable shop.

The thought crossed my mind that this discount offer may be worth the effort to look into. Once the insurance companies got wind of our little mishap, the cost of repairs and deductibles would only signal the beginning of my dread. After that, Mike and I would have to face our insurance rates going up, as I was clearly at fault. Secretly, however, I felt the blame should be shared with Constance Birdsboro and Biddy for their dual roles in displaying a stellar lack of patience.

In addition, I did not look forward to the issue of convincing Constance Birdsboro to allow her precious Mercedes to be worked on by none other than a very reputable, well-known (and more than likely) pricy establishment. None of those requirements would seem likely in light of the offer being presented. I could not help but think, though, it was not a good idea. In my state of mind, it did not sound like a completely bad proposition either. Obviously, I needed rest.

I did not have long to entertain that thought, or any other, as Biddy had just ended a telephone call with Ernst. She looked up at the two men and asked, "Hey, these guys you're talkin' 'bout, would any of 'em go by the name of Jimmy Earl?"

When flashing back to the story Biddy had described to me about the family who had exposed her to endless hours of "blurred photos, white lightening, a pile of fishin' line and a pile a sumpin'" — it was all I could do to keep from laughing out loud.

After a few moments of quite conversation between the two men, they clarified to Biddy that the name Jimmy Earl did not ring a bell. There was a fellow by the name of Clyde Earl, they both recalled, who had worked there back when the place first opened. The larger of the two men announced, "He was, by all accounts, one hell of a mechanic. Unfortunately, he had met with a terrible accident."

The taller of the two men said:

> Somehow, nobody knows for sure and ain't
> nobody knew how either, but a car he was
> working under fell on his legs. It broke one leg
> in lots of little pieces. The other leg was
> crushed so bad, they had to cut it off.

Biddy and I looked up at him at the same moment and then turned to each other, clearly with a grimace on our faces.

He tore off a wad of chew, and after using his dirty, oily finger to stuff it deep into the pocket of his cheek, he continued with:

> Story went something like, Clyde Earl was a real
> woman's man. Out carousing 'till all hours of
> the night. Lots o' times he'd show up to work
> next day still with a snoot full. That weren't
> such a problem with the other mechanics, 'cuz
> he always did real good work. It did cause a
> real mess and a lot a grief for him with his wife,
> Agnus. Yep, Agnus weren't no fading violet.
> No boy, she sure weren't! She had a right hook
> that a few good ol' boys knew way to well.

After saying that, he spit some of the most God-awful looking, brownish-green fluid — yuck! — straight out in front of him — right there on the street! Then he wiped almost all of that, which did not make it off of his hairy chin, with his filthy shirt-sleeve. Continuing with a twisted smile, he said:

She got all riled up at me once and come after
me, but I was a lot faster 'n her and got away.
She decided if she couldn't get me, she'd get my
truck. She kicked it with her big ol' boot and
broke my door — big ol' brute she was. We all
got to calling her Angus, like the cow, instead
of Agnus 'cuz she was a biggin, and mean, too.
Took three guys to pry my damn door open to
let me in and a whole lot a pounding to get the
size 13 boot-dent out of it.

There was a joke around the shop she couldn't
wear the pants in the family — her butt was
way too big. She didn't need to wear the pants
in the family anyway, cuz she'd just kick
anyone's ass that got in her way cuzin' her feet
was so damn big.

After saying this, he quickly looked in the direction of Constance
Birdsboro and apologized for his language.

Constance Birdsboro was standing just enough upwind and out of
range of the odors but still close enough to hear everything being
said. I could swear, at one point, I saw out of the corner of my eye
that she was making the gesture of a sign of the cross, as she bowed
her head slightly as if in the briefest of prayers. I noticed, too, that
most of her color (of what little she started with) had drained from
her perfectly made up face.

At that very moment, I felt a little sorry for Constance Birdsboro —
all of this commotion — and her car all dented and mangled too. If
only she had been a little more patient and not honked her horn. She
could have gone on to have her nails or hair done or perused the
jewelry store in the strip mall to eye her next, sparkly conquest.
Instead, here we were, a motley crowd, indeed. I could not help but
think that these two men were about as close as anyone could get to
being direct descendants of the characters in the old movie
Deliverance — and all of us waiting, together, for the police to arrive.

I looked over at Biddy and tried to assess what she might have been
thinking. Was she feeling a little sorry for Constance Birdsboro too?

Most likely not, I surmised. She was probably thinking that she got what she deserved, what with her being the pushy and impatient prig that she was — Constance Birdsboro that is — not Biddy — holding her cosmetically redesigned nose high up in the air, way too high up for Biddy. My thoughts were again interrupted, as the tall man continued:

> Yep, rumor was Agnus could fit into Clyde
> Earl's big size 13's and was out for blood with
> those big ol' boots on. She'd had it with Clyde
> Earl's philandering and was 'bout to put an end
> to it once and for all. Turns out, the car didn't
> crush just his legs. Got his man parts too, I
> heard.

After this last statement, he took a quick look in Constance Birdsboro's direction, and when he did not see any reaction he proceeded to say:

> Rumor was, she come to the shop that night to
> kick his ass all over the place, but sumpin'
> happened and the car fell on ol' Clyde Earl.

"That's an awful story." Unable to control herself, Constance Birdsboro nervously spoke up, "Just an awful story!"

"Yep it is," the heavy-set man replied.

> Funny thing is, she finally got what she wanted.
> Ol' Clyde Earl stopped his wanderings after
> that. I mean, with it all broken up and all, kinda
> wasn't much point to it anymore. If ya get my
> meanin'.

He started to add something but, in unison, Constance Birdsboro, Biddy and I all replied, "Yes, we get *your meanin'!*"

Biddy stood up, stretched her back and stated:

> You know, this Agnus person got more than
> she wanted, I bet. Ol' Clyde Earl probably
> wasn't going to quit his messin' 'round unless
> somethin' like this happened. So, here's Agnus,

she's got her man all to herself. Problem is, he
can't do to anyone, including Agnus, what got
him in all this trouble to start with. From the
sounds of it, no pills and bathtubs in the
wilderness were gonna help him after that car
fallin' on him either.

Everyone had a puzzled look as they turned to look at Biddy, except
me. I just smiled and looked down at my shoes.

Mike stayed with the kids back at Biddy's place, and Ernst got to us
just as the tow trucks were pulling away. After he checked to see if
all three of us were okay, he was about to ask Constance Birdsboro if
she needed a ride anywhere, when a black, shiny BMW pulled up
beside her. The driver got out and opened the back door for her, and
she scurried into the safety of the still-running (and from all
appearances), fully intact car. It then sped away.

Once we were back at Biddy's house, she told me the whole episode
reminded her of a bet she and Ernst had made a while back. Her
story, too, started with a panhandler's sign just like today, but it
ended quite differently.

I thought, "Wait! I'm getting ready to end the book — more stories
now?" Oh well, I guess adding one more to the list would not matter
all that much at this point.

Chapter 12

THE WAGER

After the experience with our automobile accident, the highfalutin society people and mountain folks we had met earlier that day, it took a little time to get settled and feel somewhat calmed down. Biddy invited me to follow her into the sun room. We arrived there just as the sun made its daily announcement; it was leading us into twilight.

Mike, the kids and Ernst decided the better plan would be to get a couple of take-out pizza's, as Biddy's and my shopping experience ended quite differently than we had planned. They would all be back before long.

Biddy began, "Ernst and I went shopping one morning. We both decided we wanted something more than strained broth to eat." Her head was filled with lines like these. It did not seem to matter to her if anyone laughed along with her. She derived a fair amount of entertainment from them, and that self-amusement seemed to be enough for her.

Readjusting in her seat, Biddy continued: "We entered a parking lot similar to the one you and I were in today. At the entrance, just like today, there was a man holding a cardboard sign."

I snuggled in my chair with my legs now pulled up under me. The way the day had gone, I needed to be comfortably situated; and I sensed Biddy wanted to tell this one story, on this day, in particular.

The day and its unfolding events could not have been all that easy for Biddy either, even though she did not show it. I told her earlier in the day that I felt like the whole, unfortunate event made me age a good ten years. I then asked her how it made *her* feel. She looked me straight in the eyes and said, "Not like that, for sure. If that happened to me, I'd be dead!"

Biddy began her story again:

> It all started with Ernst. He says to me, 'Look
> at this guy, bet he makes more money standing
> there with that dang sign than I do with my
> pension.' I laughed and said, 'No way, sweet
> cakes. Bet he barely makes enough to buy a
> cup a coffee — cheap cup a coffee at that.'

I glanced at Biddy, sensing that the wheels in my head were probably not turning as fast as her's. I then interrupted her to ask, "Tell me, Biddy, you bet Ernst that he could not make as much money, and he bet that he could, right?" She replied, "Well, O, you got some of it right. Now wait, let me tell ya what happened next."

Readjusting myself in my chair with my antenna up (just in case she was leading me into another one of her mischievous lairs), she explained, "You know, O, that man and me, we've made all kinds a bets — all our lives with each other. Proud to say, I usually win 'em." I did not doubt that Biddy had won most of the bets between the two of them, and hoped that my obvious lack of surprise did not appear to be borne from boredom.

Biddy leaned forward looking squarely into my eyes, "Here he is, my Ernst. He's saying this panhandler probably makes as much — no, more than Ernst did with his pension. So, what do I say?" Even if I could have come up with an answer, it would not have mattered. Biddy had already started in again, before I could open my mouth.

> He says, more — Ernst does. I say, no way.
> The only way a panhandler could make more
> than you do on your pension would be if it
> were a gal — a gal selling her goods! Now
> there's a bet worth makin'.

I gasped, "Oh Biddy, please tell me you didn't try to sell your goods, as you so indelicately put it. Please Biddy — Biddy?"

A picture stood clearly in my mind's eye — this little bit of a woman standing on a street corner in whatever attire she would have thought appropriate for this most inappropriate activity to — in Biddy's own words — "sell her goods." The image was something I still try, most often unsuccessfully, to avoid visualizing.

> Heaven's, O, you should know me well enough
> by now to know that, that's exactly what I
> did! — yep, I did. I say, 'Ernst, you get you
> some cardboard and make your sign. I'll get
> myself all decked out, pick a corner of a street,
> and we can put this bet to a real test.'

I was laughing and shaking my head saying, "No — Oh God, Biddy. Do I even want to hear what's next?"

Without one breath taken, Biddy spoke up, "Hell yeah, O, you want to know. If ya didn't, you'd be out a here already!" Her point made, Biddy, still laughing continued:

> So off to his shop Ernst headed with a big felt
> pen in one hand and a cardboard box, he' d
> found in the Christmas closet, in the other. I
> store good to keep boxes, O, and there he
> found one. The perfect size to cut up for his
> sign or, as he put it, his new 'want ad'!

With that last comment, we both busted out laughing.

The sun had all but set now. Still, the room felt aglow from our bright and hearty laughter. I could not help but reflect on the fact that these were some of my favorite times: Biddy and I — she, regaling me with another one of her stories — and I, just listening and being engulfed by it — the two of us, together, in my most favorite room — *anywhere.*

Biddy stood up and turned on a tall, stand-up light in the corner of the room. It was placed in such a way that I had never really paid any attention to it. Its location, whether deliberate or not, seemed to be hidden. It stood behind a tall, fully leafed Fiddle Leaf Ficus which stood happily in the corner where the window and wall connected.

Once the light was turned on, the room took on a whole new appearance. Biddy's placement of her indoor plants (in varying sizes and textures with the light illuminating behind them) made the

ambience in the room even more cozy and warm — a perfect place
to tell a story — an even better place to be told one.

Biddy, sitting back down, now carried on telling her story:

> I tell Ernst, I got some fancy high-heels I ain't
> worn in a long time. This be a good time to get
> some use out of 'em. And, I got a nice black
> dress I saved from years back, too. 'Good
> thing I kept my figure, ain't it, Ernst,' I ask.
>
> I don't get any response 'cuz he's headin' back
> downstairs to finish his sign. So, I'm a
> rummagin' 'round in some old boxes in the
> closet 'til I find the dress I was looking for —
> and then some slinky, black nylons too.

"Oh Biddy," I exclaimed while playfully raising my eyebrows and
tilting my head, "You wild girl"!

Biddy's expression changed instantly, and I could see a devilish, much
younger woman in her eyes.

"You know it, darlin'," she said with a surprising, deep-toned
giggle —

"Ernst and I used to go out quite a bit, and we'd dance the night
away, we did. Can't tell now, with his limp 'n all, but we were quite
the pair." Her lips looked almost girlish in that moment. They were
posed in a pout, mixed with being somewhat puckered, as if ready for
a gentle kiss. It was obvious to me that whatever memory had come
back to her, her eyes could not hide that it was one she cherished
deeply.

Not breaking her concentration, Biddy delved right back into her
story:

> The dress and the nylons were in good shape.
> That's why I never threw them away. I don't
> throw much away, especially if it ain't broke.
> That's why we ain't — broke that is.

Biddy's head tilted back as she let out a robust laugh.

"Get it, O?" Biddy asked in a gleeful tone.

"I sure do Biddy." I knew what she meant. It was not always easy to do, but I made the effort to be resourceful. I knew that "the dollars go a lot further when one watches the pennies." I had heard that saying sometime in my childhood and chose to adopt and carry that theory with me into my adulthood. By all the evidence she presented, it would appear Biddy held true to that same theory. And with that, she proceeded:

> Now, I tell Ernst, come 'round and pick me up
> in the car. I just got to put on some lipstick.
> He says to me, 'Biddy, are you sure this is what
> you want to do?' Well hell, not so sure, but I
> made a bet and I ain't no welcher.
>
> Next thing you know, he comes sauntering in
> wearing old pants he used to paint in and some
> old shirt with holes and tears he uses to wash
> the cars with. And the shoes — God, O, the
> shoes! Still don't know where he dug them up
> at, but they were 'bout as decrepit as we are
> now!

Biddy laughed heartily. We both did as she described the events:

> We get in the car and head to town. I'm
> figuring if we really went through with this, one
> thing or another was gonna happen. Either I
> was going to get no offers, or I'd get arrested. I
> looked over at Ernst and said, 'You know, you
> could just give up and admit I'd a won this bet,
> if we went through with it.' Ernst looks over at
> me and starts to laugh. He says, he don't
> believe me for a minute. He says even if he did
> give in, I wouldn't. And besides that, he says he
> ain't gonna quit now, not after getting all *dressed
> down* and with his big ol' sign made and all.
> Then, he looks over at me and says 'You look
> like a million.' I didn't bother to ask — 'a
> million what?'

Then, he looked down at my legs in those
fancy, black nylons and patted my thigh. I told
him to keep his eyes on the road and his hands
on the wheel — unless he had some sizable
bills. I weren't giving it away! Not today,
anyway.

"Long story short, probably too late for that now," Biddy chuckled
and said:

Anyway, we get to the place where we're gonna
do this goofy thing, and there he stands with
his ridiculous sign that says, 'Please help. Lost
my job. My dog bit me, and my wife left me.'
Pathetic, I tell ya, O. I shook my head and
headed down the street a few dozen yards away.
Pathetic, he looked.

While searching 'round for my get up, I'd found
a long, glittery cigarette holder with a fake
cigarette in it. I had used it a long time back as
part of a Halloween costume. It really added to
the look, I thought. With that in one hand and
a sequined purse in the other, which I'd started
swinging absent mindedly, I acted like I was
chewing a big wad of gum. Standing on that
corner in that way, I thought I looked more
convincing. I gotta say, I was a might pleased
with myself too. I only stumbled a couple of
times in those confounded high heels. Thought
that made me look tipsy, which might just add
to the appeal.

By now, everyone had returned, and Mike put the pizzas on the table.
Ernst asked me what story was Biddy telling now. Once Biddy told
him, he said, "Let's all sit in on this one."

My boys laid down on the floor eating their pizza, while Mike sat
next to me. Ernst sat across from us with Biddy at his side. Bella
climbed up and sat next to me in my chair. After she had eaten one
and one-half pieces of pizza, she climbed up a little more to curl up

in my lap. Biddy swallowed her last bite of pizza, and after using her napkin to wipe her lips, she said:

> Now, Ernst looked pretty silly with his sign and
> all. I, on the other hand, looked pretty damn
> good. Even so, I started to feel this whole
> thing was gettin' ridiculous. We'd agreed to try
> this stunt for an hour and then count our
> offerings. Of course, in my case, I was only
> going to report what I was offered. No way
> was I going to follow through with anything. I
> mean, there's my husband right down the
> street. Anyway, Ernst said he would have to
> beat someone to death with his sign if anyone
> tried anything. I got quite a laugh out of
> that — remember Ernst? I mean, come on —
> beat someone to death with a cardboard sign?
> I'd probably die laughing watching you try.
> Such a display that would have been!

I looked in Ernst's gentle eyes and saw the sparkle Biddy had told me about some time ago. That sparkle, she said, had caught her attention when they first met; and that same sparkle had kept her around for the several decades they had been together afterwards.

"Did you tell O what you were wearing dear?" Ernst questioned.

"Oh yes, she knows. And she knows about the cigarette holder too," Biddy answered quickly.

Mike piped up, "I didn't know you smoked, Biddy."

"I don't," Biddy replied.

Mike turned to look at me with a curious expression on his face. In response, I simply shook my head as if to say, "I will tell you later." He nodded in affirmation.

I had grown to really appreciate the silent language partners share. Once you know someone well enough, a look is all it takes to convey any number of messages. Times like these, where everything seems to fit —the kids, Mike and I together — that is what secures the family. I could not imagine being with anyone else and, in that moment, knew I would never want to be.

Biddy jumped back in:

> Ernst set the timer on his watch, and we nodded to each other; and that is when the games began — well, not really, as there were no cars for about eight minutes — after which about twenty or thirty cars went by. Not a one acknowledged either of us.
>
> It was just about near the hour's end when a car pulled up to me, and a man asked if I needed help. I said, 'No thanks. I'm just trying to win a bet.' He gave me a funny look. Once I explained what I was doing, he shook his head and his faced got all scrunched up. Without saying anything else, he sped away. Sometimes folks are just way too serious.
>
> There were several men that yelled out some pretty nauseating suggestions, but the one that seemed to be a little bit more than interested wanted to know if I would call him 'Russel.' So, I ask him if that's his name. He says for the next hour it would be. Then he added that he wanted to wear nothing more than a diaper. His final request and instruction was that I spank him with a rubber doll covered in oil. He pointed next to himself on the passenger seat. There, next to him was a rubber doll — all gooey lookin' and shiny. Reckon' he'd already slicked it up.

Upon hearing this last description, I immediately jerked my head in Mike's direction. The expression on his face would be hard to describe — and, it is one, I will never forget.

Now that Mike and I are some distance from that time and place, I often find myself laughing out loud about that incident; but certainly, I did not laugh then — no, *absolutely not then*. In fact, in a split second, we both looked at our boys laying on the floor to see what their expressions were. Simultaneously, both of us breathed a sigh of relief, when we saw that they were both fast asleep; just as their little sister had been for a while by then — asleep, curled up and cuddled in my lap.

Whether Biddy was aware if the kids were asleep, when she told that part of her story, or not, we do not know. She continued on as if nothing she had said was, in any way, out of the ordinary or might have been construed as odd or deeply disturbed.

Without so much as a pause, Biddy proceeded:

> It was my opinion, this was as good a place as any to segue into the reason why I was standing on the street corner — now appearing to be quite seductive.
>
> When I finished explaining why I was doing what I was doing, the man with the doll muttered that *I* was disgusting; and he threw a quarter at me as he yelled out, 'Get off the street, *bitch!*' Then he peeled out and sped away.
>
> Right then, I looked down the street and saw someone handing Ernst something before they, too, drove off. I whistled the ear-drum-piercing whistle my father taught me, more than half-a-dozen decades before, to get Ernst's attention. As soon as he looked at me, I gave him the time-out sign and began to wobble myself his way, on my way-too-high heels.

"You sure looked great that day, hon. I always loved that dress. But, then, I think you are beautiful in everything you wear." Ernst leaned over, and Biddy leaned into his kiss.

That tender scene would have been one of those "*aww*" moments, if I could have only cleared the picture out of my mind of some pervert in nothing more than a diaper, with Biddy spanking the creepy guy with an oily rubber doll. If this story was true, what were the odds anyone would come up with such a deranged idea? If the story was fiction — only another one of Biddy's games against reality — how did she come up with such deranged thoughts? I thought, really, what does go on up there, referencing directly to the workings of her mind.

"So how did this little bet end?" Mike asked with more urgency in his voice than one would expect under normal circumstances. What was clear to both Mike and me was that this occurrence would not have been considered, on any level, a normal circumstance. I strongly sensed that Mike wanted this particular story to end before any one of our kids may have awakened.

The thought of how to explain what was really going on in this story to any of our children was something Mike did not want to deal with, a sentiment of which I strongly concurred. We are so often on the same page, Mike and I — another reason, I am eternally grateful.

"Well that's kind of funny, Mike," Biddy piped up.

> We got to our car and Ernst hands me a wad of cash. My eyes widen and I say, 'What the hell? How much is here?' And Ernst says to me that he doesn't remember and tells me to count it. I'm sitting in the car on the ride home; and I had to count the money three times, before I could believe it!

Excited now, I asked, "Wow Biddy, how much was there?"

"Sixty-four smack-a-roos! I couldn't believe it. The damnedest thing ever!" Biddy's voice had risen.

"Sixty-four dollars and twenty-five cents to be exact, Biddy," Ernst corrected.

Biddy answered, "Yeah, that's right, dear. Our bet was for twenty-five cents. And that's exactly what I made, from that oily doll guy!"

"I have to ask you two, do you still make bets like that one?" Mike looked at me as I asked this question. His expression said, "Don't ask her that!"

Ernst and Biddy looked at each other quite seriously, searching the other's face for anything that might help trigger any memory that could help them answer my question. After a few moments, they both looked at Mike and then at me:

"Can't quite remember another bet like that one; but no, we don't make too many bets anymore. I sure don't start 'em, if we do." Looking in Biddy's direction, Ernst concluded, "We got a lot of that kind of thing out of our system a long time ago."

"Speak for yourself," Biddy interjected, "I saved that sign. I still have those heels, and I still fit into that dress!"

Before Mike and I pulled onto our street that night, I asked him if he thought any of the story we had heard earlier was true. He reached over to take my hand which was resting on my leg. Once in his hand, he gently squeezed it.

"Not for a moment." He sounded so sure of himself. I had to admit, I was pretty sure too — not one-hundred percent, mind you, but almost. I believed it was an attempt on Biddy's part to lighten the weight of all that had transpired earlier that day. It was the sickest story I could remember her telling, as of that date. If it was just that, a story, I could not help but ask, "What in the hell went on in that little woman's mind? And, God, why?" The funniest thing to me, though, was that it would not surprise me — either way. And too, as lurid and abhorrent as the thought that her story may be true; for some reason, it did not seem to matter so much to me — only because, I reasoned, Biddy was telling it.

Now, the question I asked myself was whether I was going to include this little ditty of a story in the book or not. I knew that I had more than enough material to complete it. I was too tired to decide then. All I could think about was falling into a deep sleep, in Mike's arms.

Being that self-discipline is not a trait I was gifted with, I knew that even so, it was time for me to attempt to do what I had agreed to do all along. I knew, too, I could listen to Biddy's stories for as long as she wanted to tell them. And, I knew that for as long as she was alive, she would continue to do just that. Even so, I made a commitment that it was time to — as Biddy would so often have put it — "shit, or get off the pot."

Chapter 13

WRITING A BOOK

Looking up at my desk calendar one afternoon, I almost found myself in a state of shock — shocked at all the weeks, months and seasons, too, that had passed. How could writing a book have taken so long?

Life as I had known it before the book meandered on to a somewhat normal beat. I was just not completely involved in it. Sure, I went through the motions, but my mind was elsewhere. Formulating, formatting, organizing and re-organizing, editing and re-writing had all become a way of life. No, they had become *my* life. I would go to sleep thinking about the book. I would dream about the book. I would awaken to thoughts about the book. There were times I believed that I was the book.

Then, on a Tuesday morning — it was on a Tuesday at 7:21 a.m., to be precise — I clicked on "Save" in my word-processing program for the last and final time. I exhaled a long and deliberate breath. The book was done.

*****

Looking up at the various people on Old 32, I saw that some were sitting, quietly reading their morning newspaper. Some people were talking on their cell phones, and some stood in place looking out of the windows. My hope for the latter was that they could decipher some of what they saw, as Old 32 sped along. There were a few people looking down at the floor, as if they were in deep thought; or maybe, they were completely devoid of any thought at all. There were two riders which, I had assumed, were napping as evidenced by the bobbing of their heads hung down — or their necks were broken, and they were left for dead. Wait — was that me — thinking like Biddy? If they were alive, I could not help but think that they were either extraordinarily brave or completely unaware of the possible danger. If their necks were not broken yet, the possibility lurked ahead, as Old 32 bumped and bounced along at tooth-loosening speeds.

Still observing, some of the people riding on Old 32 looked to me like they wore a look of boredom. Then again, some looked tired while others just had blank expressions on their faces. None-the-less, all wore facial expressions. None of these people were looking at me, so no one saw the expression on my face. Not being able to see it myself, I clearly knew it was an expression of pure exhilaration. *I had done it.* I had finished the book!

I had little time to absorb the reality of my accomplishment or what my next move would be, as Old 32 slammed to a complete stop. As jarring as that stop was, I was not unnerved by it; instead, I found myself awash in the glow of exuberance. Barely able to control my eagerness to print out the first copy and present it to Biddy, I thought, "She would have to like it, right?"

Whoa! Wait a minute. Up until that moment, I had not entertained the idea of the possibility that Biddy may not like the book. As that thought slashed its jagged, cruel way across my mind, I felt my stomach churn; and immediately, I felt nauseous. Seriously? "Why now," I asked myself. Why could I not have this one, fulfilling moment last for more than one moment?

I knew how Biddy could react when she was displeased about something; and I knew fully well, that I did not want that to happen with my book. I noticed, too, how my perceived possession of the book changed with the increased amount of time that I spent writing it — changing back and forth between "this" book, "our" book and "my" book.

Facing the possibility of the outcome that Biddy may not like the book, I was not surprised that I considered the book to be in the "my book" category. This was so typical of me — so damn typical — to think this way. This time, however, my thinking made me mad — really, very mad.

While biting my lower lip, I thought to myself — this is just splendid. If Biddy did not like the book, the possession of it fell to me. In turn, if she did like it, then it would be either "our" or "this," or even, "her's" — but never, "mine." When would I ever be free of my own, dogged put-downs of myself?

After stepping down off of Old 32, I maneuvered my way through the crowds of people who, by all appearances, were heading to the same big and old gray building, I was heading to. I then made my way up to my floor and to my desk. Barely noticing anyone or anything around me, I had not even expressed my usual, morning pleasantries. The pleasantries, normally exchanged, tuned into my auto-pilot public-persona station. That morning, the reception was not just bad, there was no signal at all.

Once in my chair, I turned around so no one could see my face, and I stared at the wall. I did not know how long I sat there — seconds? a brief, few moments? half of an hour?

I turned my chair back around. Then, ever so slowly — from left to right — I perused the entire space that housed mine and everyone else's cubicles.

The same, old and predictable activities were in motion, as they had always been each and every morning that I had worked there; although on this morning, there was something just a little different. Everyone was performing their routine activities — those activities were all unfolding before my eyes, like the daily mirage of the "ordinary" they had always been. So, what was different, I wondered.

In a few, short minutes, I realized that the rush of anger in me had disappeared. My blood pressure had returned to normal, and even though I could see everything happening around me, I did not hear the sounds that should have been clearly connected to the actions — that was exactly what it was! The sounds that should go with the actions were missing. Once I realized that this was what the difference was, I heard a voice in my head say, "You've got this. You've done it. Get on with it!" The voice I heard was Biddy's. Her voice grew louder until what happened next was so shocking, it made me jerk back in my chair. As it turned out, what happened next was my realization that it was *not* Biddy's voice at all. The voice I was hearing was my own.

My voice continued to repeat, "You've done it! Now get on with it. Get it published!" My voice was strong, full of confidence, forceful and deliberate. Upon this realization, I said out loud in barely a whisper, "Well, hot damn. I thought for sure, it was Biddy." I felt my cheeks warming, as I began to smile.

The time was well after midnight the next morning, when I finished printing Biddy's copy of the book. I would take it to her that evening. Printing out the book did not take that long, but my reviewing everything over and over again did take extra time, a lot of time.

Earlier that same night, Mike came to me looking a bit disheveled, as he had just woken up. He sat down next to me encompassing both of my hands in his. His were the hands I had come to know and trust more than any other person's in my life. He then looked directly into my eyes and asked, "What else can you do to this book that you haven't already done?" Only then, did I realize that procrastination was no longer a viable option.

*****

When I knocked on the door of Biddy and Ernst's house and no one answered, I asked myself, "Did I come all this way to the island to have to turn around and build up my nerve to come back at another time?" There was no way I was going to leave the book on their porch. Just as I turned to leave, Ernst came around from the back-side of the house and called up to me.

"Hey there, O. Didn't know you were here." I waved to him and started down the stairs. He explained,

> I'm so sorry you had to make this trip for nothing, O. Biddy got a call from a neighbor in need of a ride and won't be back for quite a while yet. You can leave the book with me if you like.

I was surprised at how relieved I felt. I could leave the book with Ernst instead of coming back to give it to Biddy. He would see that she got it. I replied, "Oh, that would be great Ernst. Then you can start it first." He responded abruptly,

"Not on your life, O. She'd have my hide. She said no one, and she meant *no one* but you and her get to read it first." To which I replied,

"Really? I have got to admit it, Ernst, I'm a wreck over whether she will like it or not."

Ernst had that sparkle in his eyes when he looked into mine. He took the copy of the book from my hands and put his hand on my shoulder. He said very slowly and softly, "She will love it, just like she loves you."

For a brief second, I felt I could not breathe. Neither of us, Biddy nor I, had ever said anything about love before. Having heard it said out loud, I now knew that Biddy felt for me, the way I already knew; that I felt for the both of them. And, in that instant, I believed everything would be okay.

"Tell her to call me when she has finished it, please. Thank you, Ernst." I turned to go, when Ernst said, "Wait a minute, O."

I turned to see him holding the book against his chest. He had an expression on his face like one would expect to see on the face of a loving grandfather.

"No, thank *you*, O. You've been, no all of you have been, a wonderful surprise in our lives — something for which we'll always be grateful."

My smile must have said all that he needed to hear. He winked at me, turned around and walked back into the side yard and out of my sight.

It was not until I had driven halfway back to the ferry, when I realized that my cheeks were wet from tears — not from sadness, but from relief. After so much time and so much effort, I felt a weight lifted from me. No matter what happened next, I knew I had put all of myself into this project. Whether the book would sell or not sell — and if it did sell, or if the critics were harsh — I knew I had done what I said I would do. I had fulfilled a lifelong dream — no, I had fulfilled two lifelong dreams — one for Biddy and one for me. I had set a goal and reached it. I liked the feeling of accomplishment that gave me. And, more than that, *I liked the book.* I liked the way that made me feel, too; and for the first time in a long time, if ever, *I liked me.*

And, to think, all that it took to help me to get there was my bonding with an outspoken, sometimes cranky, little old woman with a quick wit, a kick-ass sense of humor; and, whether she knew it, or would ever admit to it, a great big heart.

Whatever may have happened on that day we first met — Biddy, in her hurried fashion going about her busy day, and I, performing my daily, non-descript and boring job — was that I *did* pull the lucky number, Number 221, to be exact.

In gathering all the information Biddy offered me, I had accomplished something she had wanted to do for most of her life. In that process, I garnered the strength to go forward with something I had only dreamt about doing. I knew, too, that our relationship — Biddy's and mine — had become one symbiotic in nature and, no less true, if fate truly existed and had, in its own way, intervened.

Chapter 14

THE CALL

In all of the time I had known Biddy, we had never gone for more than three days without a telephone call or visit; so when one week turned into two with no word from her, the waiting became unbearable. I found it almost impossible to function on any level other than being on automatic pilot. Mike did all he could to comfort me, as he could see that the waiting was taking its toll on me.

At first, I could not help but reflect on how relieved I was to have completed the book. Then, the anticipation of giving it to Biddy to read, well, that anticipation was barely livable — and now, the waiting. *God*, I am not good at waiting. Waiting to me could be compared only to a cruel diet: a diet which I would be forced to stay on with absolutely no possibility of ever breaking away from; and, the option to stuff a whole chocolate cake into my mouth simply would not exist.

Then, on the sixteenth day following my dropping off of the book and still no word from Biddy, I saw on my telephone display, that Ernst had called while I was in the shower. This situation was somewhat reminiscent of the time when Biddy had the flu (quite a while back) and could not talk without coughing. She had Ernst call me to let me know, so I would not worry. Actually, that is not entirely true. This is what really happened:

I received a call from Ernst. He explained to me that he was letting me know that Biddy would not be able to talk for a few days, as she was trying to coax a pervert out of her closet. She believed, if it was anything like the last time this happened, it could take some time. He went on to say in his calm and gentle way, "Not to worry, O."

I was so shaken by Ernst even mentioning the word "pervert," it took me some time to adjust my mind. When it came to Biddy, I was never completely sure what was one-hundred-percent true or false — or, what was a mad combination of any number of percentages that her story was based in reality, or just in *her* reality. I had to take the bait and so I asked, "What was a pervert doing in her closet?" Ernst gently replied, "Sucking on his toes."

Well, hell, of course he was! Sure, I should have guessed that, right? A significant amount of time had passed, before I found out that Biddy had caught the flu. That explanation would have been too easy, and it lacked "the different colors of life." That was something she would remind me of so often. "The different colors of life" she would reiterate, "is something we all need to pay more attention to." By all accounts, the different colors of life in Biddy's head would make a psychedelic whirlwind look pale.

So much of Biddy's and my relationship involved the forced evolution of my adjustment to that which is different. The foreign — foreign to my normal — foreign to most people's normal — was pretty much status quo when it came to Biddy. The realization came to me, after some time had passed, that the only thing I would come to expect from her was the "unexpected."

Once I saw Ernst had called, I hoped with all I had to hope with, that he had left a message. I saw none — Damn! — *no message.* With a towel wrapped around my wet hair on top of my head and with one foot threaded through one leg hole of my underwear, I hopped to the kitchen counter to get my reading glasses. The latter being something I had acquired, too, since first meeting Biddy. I needed them, so that I would be sure to hit the right telephone number to call Ernst back. My stomach kept creeping up closer to my throat, while I waited for him to answer the phone.

Finally — "Hello?" — Ernst's voice sounded different. It sounded broken and sad.

"Hello, Ernst, this is O. I see that you called me. Is everything alright?" He responded, "Yes, I did dear. I'm afraid, O, well, there's no other way to say this. I have some very sad news to report." My lungs involuntarily took in a deep breath. Ernst continued, "The last thing Biddy said was — " There is a saying, "My heart sank." It just so happened, in that moment, I felt like that was literally happening inside my body. I reached to grab the counter, as I needed to brace my body, believing I was going to pass out. All I could say, barely whispering, was, "What is it Ernst?"

Ernst replied, "Biddy wanted me to tell you," — Ernst stopped briefly to clear his throat.

> She wanted you to know, more than anyone
> else, that she went to see her doctor earlier to
> find out why, they've decided to stop giving her
> pap smears. She said she's still got all her parts!
> They may need a little oiling now and again, but
> she's still got 'em!

"What?" "What the . . . ?" It was then that my mostly naked and still wet body quivered back to reality. I stood there, as my body went from quivering to shaking.

There was a loud and raucous round of laughter coming from my phone. I stood there like a dumb, partially naked statue — a picture that I hoped to erase from my mind's eye once and forever. Still, I must admit, that is something I have yet to accomplish.

Too dumbfounded to muster anything more than a meek, "What?" again, I stood there ready to openly acknowledge, that I was quite accomplished at being a complete dolt.

Then, what I heard, between Biddy's fits of cackling, was her voice saying:

> You get the family together, and get over here.
> We've got quite the spread set up. Pack
> everybody up — bring 'em all and their
> appetites too.

Wow. What had just happened? I needed to get my bearings. In that first moment, I was so grateful and relieved. In the next moment, I was furious. Biddy had pulled so many stunts — many, where I found myself on the short-end feeling like a rube. This time, though — maybe because of all my anticipation — this time, it angered me in a way, even I was unfamiliar with.

I could not help but think of the time Biddy warned me against waxing my "private area," as she put it. It pleased me, that time, she had not assigned a name for it like "Lily Lou." I told her that I really had no intention of doing it anyway, but she insisted on continuing with the story of someone she had known that did — sadly, quite unsuccessfully.

Keeping my lunch down depends on my not going into all the details of this story. I will say, though, Biddy told me it all seemed so pointless. And the pain — this was not something she could relate to going through for a hairless, private area. She added that when you get older, a woman does not have to be concerned with too much hair down there anyway. I innocently asked, "Why? What happens to it?"

Biddy's quick reply?

> What the hell do ya think happens to it? You
> leave it on the park bench, where you go to
> drink a cheap bottle of wine you've hidden in a
> paper bag!

Though we both laughed, her's was the more joyous.

I was not sure if Biddy was serious about the loss of, or lack of, hair on an older woman. I could not help but think that if anyone would know, she would be the one. I thought Biddy may just be having one of her "let's mess with the innocent one" moments. "The innocent one" was just one of the many names she liked to call me, when she was really, very successful at fooling me. I am afraid, this occurred more often than not.

When Biddy offered to show me the hair loss she had experienced, I graciously declined. My response was simple and polite, "Thank you, no. I'll take your word for it."

I found myself at that same juncture where I had found myself on so many other occasions. This time, though, it did not feel the same. This time, I was angry. Having been fooled, time and time again, was not the problem. I was scared this time — fooled and scared — with a sadness I could not remember ever having felt. This mixture of different feelings made for a very unpleasant and unpalatable emotional concoction.

Ernst presented his comments to me in such a way as to deliberately throw me off balance — I knew that — and it worked. This time, my being so frightened that Biddy may have been, well, dead, was no laughing matter. This time, I was going to say something about it, too. My train of thought was interrupted by Biddy's voice on the other end of the telephone.

"Hey you! Did ya hear me? Bring the family over as soon as possible, we got a lot of great food. It's time we do some celebratin', O?" I responded with:

> Yes, Biddy, I am here. I have to say this one
> was nowhere near funny. You cannot think it
> was. The way Ernst was talking and what he
> was saying was meant to make me think you
> had died. That is so far from funny, Biddy. I
> am really, very angry. It was such a mean thing
> to do, and so wrong!

My voice had elevated considerably as Biddy replied:

"Oh dear, O — we were just havin' — just tryin' to have some fun. Guess we went too far, huh?" I scolded her with —

"Way too far, Biddy. My heart is still trying to recover." Biddy replied:

"Well bless your little heart, O. I guess you love me! *Aww, that's sweet.* We love you too."

When I heard her say it, I felt a little embarrassed. It was the only time Biddy had ever said anything of that nature to me. I knew in my heart that it would seem like a natural emotion to feel — especially after all of the time we had spent together and all that she and I had shared about our lives. I still did not feel any better about their cruel prank. That just rubbed me the wrong way. When someone says that they love you right after they have hurt you — it does *not* make it suddenly okay!

The anger I felt probably stemmed from the memories I had of my relationship with my parents. After going on one of their drug binges, they would come home and tell us kids how much they loved us. They were responsible enough to be sure that there was always enough food in the house when they went missing. As children, we learned early on how to take care of ourselves. So, even though we may not have been hungry for food, we were starving for our parents' attention. By the time they came home, we had learned to accept any sign of affection from them that they were willing to offer to us. I had reached a pinnacle in time, when their words ceased to mean anything to me; they had become only empty words. I, for one, would have chosen to forego ever hearing those words uttered again, if it meant that my parents would never leave us for another one of their drug-induced, blacked out weekends.

Maybe, the raw emotions I was feeling came from growing up — all of us kids — suckling the teats of temporary love. First, the hurt from being truly abandoned — then, the reward — they would come back with a simple, "We love you." Eventually, it stopped working for me. By then, the punishment and reward cycle had burrowed well into my memory resulting in my expectations of how others should engage with me. The hurt *won* over any positive feelings I may have had towards my parents, and I just said "I quit." Since then, I had little communication with either of my parents because of it. Often, I found myself wondering: "How could I lose something, I never had to begin with." And yet, I never completely closed the door on what *could be*.

Biddy was quiet on the other end of the telephone. Silent, for more time than I could ever remember her being. I spoke first, after the lull, "Biddy?"

"Yes, O."

Then, at the same time, we both said, "Listen."

I said, "You go first." She told me to do the same. This was another crossroad for me — one of the many that my life's new path would intersect.

If someone had told me what I was about to say and how I was about to say it, I would have been apprehensive. For whatever reason, the words just came out — raw, candid and non-scripted. I heard and felt it, just like Biddy did, for the first time:

> I know you love to play with me, and I guess I
> love it too. There is a point, though, that you
> have to know when to stop — a line you don't
> cross with me. This latest act crossed that line.

I do not think I swallowed or took a breath, I just continued:

"I love you both, too. I deserve to be treated with kindness and have little room left in my heart for hurt. I hope you will respect that."

The silence that followed was brief. Biddy quipped:

"You got it doll! Now, get the family packed up and over here!"

It may have seemed like no big deal to Biddy, but to me, their "little" joke was enormous. I had said something that may have felt mild, even benign to her. For me, what I said, and how I said it, was a huge accomplishment — during which time, I lost all thoughts of the book and whether or not she liked it — as well as almost losing my breakfast.

Biddy did say it was time for us to celebrate. Now, that would be a sign, from anyone else, that there was good news. However, being that Biddy said it, I would have to wait and see.

In a couple of hours, we were on the ferry heading to Ernst and Biddy's place. Mike was calm as usual, and the kids were just being kids. Between Allen poking his brother and sister (enough to make them both angry) and my starting in with threats (which rarely worked anymore), it was just like any other day on a family outing for us. Suddenly, Mike shouted out, "I just saw a whale breach!"

Everyone gasped and starting asking, "Where? Which side of the boat? Daddy, where is it? How big was it?"

Mike opened his door and instructed, "Let's all go up onto the deck where we can see better and see if we can spot it again. Maybe, we'll see a whole pod!"

Right then, nothing would have been able to stop them. Just a moment earlier, they were the World's worst enemies. Now, the three of them were giggling and eager to help each other spot the magnificent sea mammal, as they ran up ahead of us. Mike let go of my hand stating that he had to keep the herd in line and get them to slow down. I told him to go on ahead, as I pulled the hood on my sweatshirt over the top of my head. While on the ferry, the air felt cooler than on land; and there was usually a breeze, if not an outright, cold wind. That day, I felt a gentle and cool breeze picking up.

Once on the top deck, the view was nothing shy of beautiful. The water was calm. Above me, the clouds were of different shapes and sizes; their colors graduating from gray to crisp white with varying tints of blue in the sky scattered between them. The Olympics, still showing evidence of a little snow on their highest peaks, stood tall and majestic on the horizon.

Initially, it had not dawned on me that Mike may have not been totally truthful in regards to seeing a whale. Whether he had or had not, at that point, I could not see why it would have mattered. Like the little animals they were, as if they had been caged and finally set free; the kids were happy just searching the water for whales and loving the fresh air, the view, and the sense of freedom that being outdoors creates.

*****

The scent of a variety of delicious foods wafted down from Biddy and Ernst's kitchen to the driveway below. We all commented on the scrumptious aromas before we even made it out of the car. Biddy must have been cooking for days. She did that often when in her "grandiose moods," she would say. Not knowing what concoction was triggering such an olfactory source of delight, I was not just hungry — I was starving!

"Come on in!" Ernst yelled out from inside their house, as soon as he saw the kids running up the stairs.

Bella was first to reach the door. It swung open, and she was swept up in Ernst's big arms.

"Hello Bella. Bella, my little gal, that's what I call her, 'cuz she ain't no fella. My Bella pal." Ernst started this little greeting some time ago. I could see on Bella's smiling face, it was still a hit. "Plant one on me!" Ernst said next. At this, Bella gave Ernst a big kiss on his cheek. He then set her back down only to see her run on into the house looking for Biddy, where no doubt she would get a treat of sorts.

The boys were next to make it to the front door. Mike held them back just long enough to prevent the inevitable stampede they were capable of creating, had he not. Ernst met the two of them at the front door; and after high-fiving them, they, too, disappeared into the house. Mike, still getting the bottle of Biddy's favorite wine out of the car, told me to go on ahead.

Ernst, holding the door open for me, smiled that warm, gentle smile. In the sweetest of voices, he whispered to me, "She made me do it." This was followed by a big hug. And then he remarked, "She's in the sun room waiting for you." I turned around to seek out Mike. He was ready for me, as usual. He gave me a "thumbs-up" gesture and I, too, disappeared into the Biddsworth abode.

Once inside, like most mothers would do, I took inventory of where my kids were and what they were doing. I had no reason to be concerned; Ernst had started leading them into the backyard, where I could see smoke rising from his outside grill. With some trepidation, I made my way to the sun room.

Biddy stood at the end of the table in my favorite room, the room we had spent hundreds of hours in — listening, recording, talking and sharing so much of our lives. She stood with her back to me; and by all appearances, she was looking out at and enjoying the glorious view. She then turned and faced me.

I was not sure what she was holding in her hands; however, after a couple of seconds, I could see that it was a small, graduation cap — the kind one wears when they graduate from high school or college, only this cap was one-half the size of the usual cap used for such an event. How odd, I thought, that Biddy was holding the hat upside down, until I saw that there was a card under a rectangular-shaped box sitting in the middle of it.

I felt overwhelmed — perhaps because of the way the day had unfolded; or maybe, because I was finally going to find out what Biddy thought of the book — probably, a combination of both those scenarios. I felt as if I was not completely in my own body, let alone in the room. Then, Biddy outstretched her arms to hand me the upside-down graduation cap.

"So, what is this, Biddy?" I asked, as I took the cap from her and looked down into it.

> I have to say, O, this is a big day. This little gift
> is from Ernst and me. After reading your
> book, we both feel you have graduated from a
> 'Wanna be writer' to a 'You're a real writer and a
> damned good writer' status!

I looked inside the hat one more time and then back at her, thinking I would see Biddy's face. Instead, I saw the back of her head, as she had turned back around to face the windows again.

"Wow, Biddy . . . from a 'want-to-be writer' to a 'you-are-a-writer' status, does that mean you liked the book?" I felt a slight quiver in my voice, as I asked her the question.

> Liked the book, O? Hell no, in all honesty, I
> didn't like it. *I loved it.* Never knew I was such
> an interesting character! Told Ernst to hold on
> to the three hairs on the top of his head, 'cuz
> we be gettin' calls from Hollywood! Someone
> is gonna want to meet this Old Biddy to see
> which actress should play her!

She burst out with such a laugh, I could not control my laughter either.

Biddy often said, "Laughter was contagious among most people who have their heads screwed on right." She made it clear to me, that there were some very real "sick-a doos" as she referred to them, and "Nothin' could make 'em laugh — well, almost nothin'." She was sure they would get a kick out of some "best-left-unmentioned" circumstances.

Biddy lived by the rule, that life in this world would be better; if more people laughed and found joy in the little things:

Everybody's expectin' everythin' to go their way
all the time — downright selfish, I say. What a
bunch a whiney wieners, we got. Folks gotta
lighten' up. And while we at it, how's 'bout not
just working on laughter? How's 'bout we
make it so not just colds, the damn flu and
STD's is the only things that be contagious?
How about makin' love contagious too!

I could not argue with any of Biddy's advice. She had always made
her points clear and, sometimes, in ways I could actually repeat. For
a "grouchy old crotch," as she referred to herself on occasion, she
made some deep and heartfelt observations.

Coming back into the "now" of where we were at, I thought she liked
the book. *She really did like it!* All of the heavy weight of my worry of
whether she would like it or not just fell away. I had done what I said
I would do, and I did it to my main character's — my star's —
satisfaction. For me that was big, really, *very big.*

"Open the box girl, hurry up, before everyone else invades our
space." Biddy's face lit up like a kid at Christmas. That felt special to
me — Biddy wanting this moment to be shared just between the two
of us.

After setting the graduation cap down on the table, I retrieved the
box from it. Nothing came to my mind as to what could have been
in it. I guess my face gave away that fact as, just then, Biddy laughed
yet again.

"For God's sake, O, open the damn thing! I'm not gettin' any
younger!"

"Okay, okay — Jesus, what's the race? Gear down!" I instantly
looked over at her, as my comment sounded like something she
would have said. Not me — no, no — it was oh so very *not*
something "O" would have said. But there it was — no denying it.
Those words came straight out of my own mouth.

Her face lit up even more, as the words spewed from her lips —
almost as if she was out of breath: "And, there it is. I've done it.
I've passed down my genes!"

One would have thought that Biddy had won an amazing prize, what with the expression on her already, overly excited face. Leave it to Biddy to like the fact, that I would have said something so purely out of character for me — and more like her.

To be honest, during the process of writing the book, I caught myself (on more than one occasion) thinking a thought or saying a phrase that could easily have come straight out of Biddy's mind, or mouth.

When two people spend so much time in each other's company, it is not so peculiar; that, either person may have influenced the other's behavior to some degree. I could not help but reflect on whether any part of my personality may have influenced her. I strongly doubted that. There it was again — my daily dose of negativity towards myself. Taking that into account, "Why," I asked myself, "would a strong-willed, very in-control woman such as Biddy have a need to acquire any traits from a person such as I?"

"Wake up, O! Dammit, open the box! NO! Open the card first." Biddy's insistence shook my brain back to the present — literally and figuratively. Her eagerness for me to open both the card and the gift exceeded the level of excitement my kids would have displayed while waiting for me to open a gift from any one of them.

Startled out of my thoughts, I pulled the slim, blue ribbon from the box; and, just as I started to lift the top off, Biddy yelled at me again, "No, O, you silly girl. *Read the card first!*"

I reached into that section of my purse — excuse me, my satchel — where my reading glasses were kept — no glasses. That was so odd. I was sure that I had put them back there earlier in the day. There were several, different compartments in the particular satchel, I had brought with me on that day. I opened each one of them, performing the frustrating process of elimination, searching for the blasted things. They were nowhere to be found.

I laid everything out on the table, as I pulled each item; so I would not have to keep moving things out of my way. I found a baseball, a measuring tape and two pairs of sun glasses with one missing a lens. Neither pair would have helped me to read, as they did not contain prescription lenses. I then pulled out my wallet, a hair brush, blush, lipstick, a broken pencil, two pens, a worn-out emery board and what appeared to have been, at one time, a pack of chewing gum with a lot of lint stuck to it — oh, and one of Bella's socks which was more than likely the source of the lint — but no reading glasses.

I told Biddy that I had wished I could read the card, but I did not have my reading glasses with me. Biddy immediately reached behind her and picked up her own.

These were Biddy's glasses: the ones that I had never kept it a secret of how much I loved; and, the glasses with the gold rims and rhinestones that she wore the first time we met. Now, held in her hand, she handed them to me: "Hurry, O, use these."

I took the glasses from Biddy, and when I put them on, they were so strong; I had to readjust my stance to prevent myself from falling backwards.

"Okay, wow, these are a lot stronger than mine." I said this while regaining my balance:

> You just wait dear. Not your time yet. You'll
> get there, O — not too soon, I hope. When
> you do, though, I'll have been gardenin' — you
> know, helpin' push up 'em daisies for a good
> spell by then. I hope not to be a gardenin' too
> soon, mind ya. I plan on being 'round for
> another century or two. It'll have to be
> sometime after that.

At that point, Biddy looked away from me. I could still see her reflection in the window; and her cheeks were definitely in the "smile" mode — oh, so, Biddy!

I knew, since becoming involved with Biddy and Ernst (he being the main character in Biddy's life and her biggest fan as well as her closest cohort in most, if not all, of her diabolical schemes), I was still confused more often than a rational thinking person may think I should be. Add to that, the cast of characters I had been introduced to: some that were notably interesting; and, some others ranging from strangely odd to quite bizarre. My brain had gone through an extraordinary growth period. Anyone may seem confused under these conditions. That was the story I told myself, and I was sticking to it.

Early on in our relationship, I had discovered that my facial expressions, when around Biddy and Ernst, fell into two main categories: one, of bewilderment and the other, of abject confusion. I must have worn both faces on that day, as I stood in that sun room; all the while, Biddy's glasses were making me dizzy.

> Oh, for dammed sakes, O! Get your head back
> down here with the rest of us, and open the
> dammed card. And, if you want to know what
> the hell's in the box, you're gonna have to open
> it to find out!

Biddy then turned on her heels and headed towards the kitchen. I stood with the box in my still opened hand and watched her continue out into the back-yard, where everyone had already gone. Biddy was not known for her exemplary connection to patience.

Standing in *the* room — my favorite room, *anywhere* — I knew instinctively that whatever was in the box, it had to be good. Biddy was just too excited for it not to be.

A typical "Biddy" ploy was the buildup. She enjoyed luring me to the bait, watching me bite and then playing me for just as long as she was entertained. Sometimes, she would play me for quite a while. Other times, she would grow tired of it all and cut me loose. Sometimes, that could be relatively early into the game. Her inconsistency was consistent.

I looked down at the card and the box through Biddy's nauseatingly strong glasses. "The card first," she had instructed. It was simply addressed to "O."

I pulled the card from the envelope and saw a picture of a rocket ship a few moments after having been launched heading up into space. On the right-hand bottom corner of the card, someone — my guess was that "someone" was Biddy — had scribbled the words, "Bon Voyage." Upon opening the card, I also saw the words scribbled, "This is your time. You're on your way to high places! Enjoy the ride." It was signed, "Biddy and Ernst." Directly under their names, it said, "We love ya!"

Seeing what the card said gave me chills. Together, we had done it. Biddy was not one for too much sentiment. What she wrote was heartfelt and touched me deeply.

When it was getting harder to see through Biddy's reading glasses, I realized it was my tears that added to the difficulty. I swallowed hard as I opened the box next.

At first, I thought that my feeling light-headed may have been just Biddy's glasses with their strong prescription lenses. More than likely, though, it was that, along with the mixture and range of emotions that I was experiencing.

I lifted off the box lid; as I did that, I heard loud applause and laughter in back of me, as I tried to grasp what I saw in the box. "What the hell?" I asked, barely audible.

Laying in the box was a pair of glasses — gold rimmed with rhinestones — just like Biddy's. I could hear the laughter and clapping in back of me, but I still felt disassociated with my surroundings.

As I slowly turned around, I saw all of them — Biddy, Ernst, Mike and all of the kids — clapping and laughing. Of course, the loudest laughter came from Biddy.

"Try 'em on, O! Hurry, see if you can see any better with those than with mine."

By this time, all of the kids had run up to me to peek inside the box.

"Oh mommy, they're beautiful. Can I try them on too?" Bella's face was glowing.

The boys were giggling as Mike said, "Let's see if you can read as well with them as you can with yours." He reached over to take Biddy's glasses from me, as he pulled out of his pocket my mysteriously missing reading glasses — no longer a mystery now.

The reality began to dawn on me; everyone must have been in on this setup. How in the world did Biddy manage to get my family to keep it a secret? I had to marvel at her accomplishment. There was not one holiday or birthday that I could remember where one or more of the kids — and that included Mike on occasion — could keep from revealing at least part of a planned surprise.

After I handed Biddy's glasses over to Mike, I took the new ones out of the box and put them on. They were perfect. They fit just right, and I could see as well with them, if not better, as I could with my normal reading glasses.

Another round of applause followed. I looked at my reflection in the window and saw little sparkles glimmering off the rhinestones. I was in love with them, *all of them* — the glasses, Biddy, Ernst, Mike, the kids — and in that moment, my whole life.

The rest of the day seemed to float by. I had lost all sense of time. We ate the best food I could ever remember Biddy making, and her cooking was always good.

The kids were having the best times of their lives playing Badminton with Mike and Ernst. Biddy and I joked with each other and even talked about *our next book*. I was completely taken by surprise, when she said that she wanted to get started on another book as soon as it would be possible.

Biddy thought that maybe we could write a series of "The Old Biddy" books as in: The Old Biddy and Politics; or, The Old Biddy and Religion. We both bent over laughing when she suggested, The Old Biddy and a Hammer!

Whatever we decided on doing, Biddy warned, "We need to get to it. My mind, like time, is a fleeting thing." I was in the game for whenever she wanted to start.

During our conversation, I ventured out of my comfort zone and asked Biddy what she thought of — after reading this first book — if she thought I could write a book, a story — one, I would create on my own. Did she think I was good enough at writing to do that? That is what I really meant. When I finally got the words out, she shot me back a look that would peel paint.

I quickly responded with, "Good. I really want to give it a try. Thanks, Biddy." She then looked directly at me and said, "Yes, O. You're ready — in every way."

*****

At one point, sometime later on that day, Ernst observed me admiring my new glasses. He took me aside to tell me that if and when my prescription may change, new lenses could be inserted into the frames of these new glasses. He explained:

> Biddy had insisted to the Optometrist that, no
> matter what happened in the future, she wanted
> to be sure that new lenses could be inserted, so
> you could always wear them; especially, since
> there are two diamonds mixed in with the
> rhinestone-encrusted rims. There is one on
> both of the right and left sides.

> 'They must be able to accommodate
> prescription changes,' she insisted. So, I asked
> her, 'What did the Optometrist say, my love?'
> And you know how Biddy responded, 'You
> mean after he was done shaking?'

Ernst and I both laughed out loud. I realized my eyes must have looked like the size of saucers when I asked, "Did you say, diamonds?"

> Sure did, O. You don't think Biddy would give
> you anything less, do ya? She always says,
> 'nothing less than the best, for the best.' The
> only thing is, I can't imagine how you'll know
> where they are. They blend in so well. We
> have to talk to the jeweler. She had one
> embedded on both the right and left side like I
> said. She just can't remember where!

I was left absent for words — a situation Biddy rarely, if ever, would find herself in.

As the day progressed into evening, I found my way back to the sun room and sat in what I now considered to be *my chair*. Looking out over the prairie and the Puget Sound, I could see the sun floating down towards the horizon. I began to reflect on all that had happened since the day I called out Number 221. My life's path intersected with Beatrice Biddsworth's on that day; and the enormity of the changes brought about in my life since that meeting would leave my mouth and mind stuttering in an effort to recall them all.

Being so immersed in something so extraordinary — in something of such a great proportion — may change one's perception of time, of who they are; and, honestly, their entire existence. As it turned out, my perception of all these things would be forever changed from writing *our* book.

I opened and read my card again. She had ended it with, "Enjoy the ride." On that day, I was doing just that: the joyous atmosphere; being enveloped in the sounds of happy voices of so many of the people I loved echoing all around me; the wonderful food; and the beautiful view. All of it gave me a true sense of peace in my heart.

In that sun room on that day, my life was warmer and fuller. I was filled with new hope and open to not only what my future had waiting for me, but what I would bring to that future too. I recognized that I was traveling on a new path and was emotionally stronger than I had ever been. This realization led me to understand, surviving a failure was possible; because now, I knew that I would continue to try.

As I watched the sun touch the edge of the earth that night, I knew my life's ship was traversing on a different trajectory than I had ever dared to dream was possible. I saw the possibilities as nothing less than amazing. And the changes in my life, well, those new footings had already begun to set.

What stood out to me as being the most amazing change was that then, as now, it was I who would be piloting the ship.

ABOUT THE AUTHOR

S. Wilbur often ponders the human race and the situation it has gotten itself into and finds that listening to or watching the news is a detriment to the melody in her mind. Writing offers her an escape from the constant barrage of noise that humankind makes, often she thinks, at their own peril.

She shares her life with her family in the Pacific Northwest and lives with her best friend and husband of several decades in their island home. They have a beautiful view of the Puget Sound which also offers an abundance of wildlife just outside their window. A vast array of bird species frequents their yard and water features yearlong which facilitates her consummate friendship with the local Anna's hummingbirds, thereby offering a bed and breakfast with a bath facility, and providing additional food to the migrating Rufus's that arrive every March.

Currently, she is working on her next two books, *Peculiar People* and *Seeking Utah*.

www.ingramcontent.com/pod-product-compliance
Lightning Source LLC
Chambersburg PA
CBHW031834170626
46807CB00004B/1460